AN AVALON ROMANCE

THE PRICE OF VICTORY
Sandra Leesmith

Sterling Wade, a successful professional cyclist, finds the one thing he's missing in life—a woman to love. But Debra Valenzuela refuses to allow a relationship with any man to interfere with her determination to become a professional cyclist.

When Debra is seriously injured during a race, her ambition and wish to succeed and win her father's love are put to the test. With Sterling at her side during her rehabilitation, Debra learns that love is not a race to be won, but something to be earned. Can Sterling help Debra follow her dream and in the process discover new purpose for his own life? Will they accept the price of victory?

THE PRICE
OF VICTORY

•

Sandra Leesmith

AVALON BOOKS
NEW YORK

Published by Avalon Books,
an imprint of Thomas Bouregy & Co., Inc.
160 Madison Avenue, New York, NY 10016

Library of Congress Cataloging-in-Publication Data

Smith, Sandra Lee.
    The price of victory / Sandra Lee Smith.
        p. cm.
    ISBN 978-0-8034-7660-8
    I. Title.
    PS3619.M5929P75 2011
    813'.6—dc22
                                2010046203

PRINTED IN THE UNITED STATES OF AMERICA
ON ACID-FREE PAPER
BY RR DONNELLEY, BLOOMSBURG, PENNSYLVANIA

To my dear husband, Ed,
who taught me the joy of bicycling

Acknowledgments

I would like to thank my critique partners, who helped me get back on track with my writing: Joan Domning, Barbara Larriva, Nancy Damato, Peggy Parsons, and Debbie Federici.

And thank you to all my "Seeker Sisters" on Seekerville, whose encouragement and dedication have been a blessing.

Chapter One

Sterling Wade sipped his ice-cold Gatorade and wove his way through the crowd. Bicyclists dressed in neon colors surged around him, pinning numbers onto the backs of their teammates or meditating before the race.

Voices buzzed. Anticipation pulsated among the throngs of cyclists and their fans. Excitement throbbed.

But not for Sterling.

What's the matter with me? Thirty minutes until the start of the race. Where was the jangle of nerves, the knot in his stomach that prepped him for the competition?

Nothing. He felt nothing.

Beads of sweat formed on his brow. Scottsdale should be cool in March. Not today. The Arizona sun beat down, heating his toned body. He gazed through the moving waves of orange, pink, red, and blue, looking for the silver shirts of his teammates.

Thump. Sharp pain shot through Sterling's hip as he crashed into the metal frame of a bicycle.

"What the—"

Horrified, Sterling swung forward, grabbing the bicycle he had bumped into. A young woman dressed in kelly green Lycra tried to free her cleated feet from the pedals and flung out an arm to regain her balance.

"Grab my hand!" Sterling reached over the handlebars but not in time.

"Catch the bike!" The woman pushed her bicycle toward him before she landed with another *thump* on the pavement.

"Are you hurt?" Sterling quickly lowered the bike and dashed around to help her up. "I was searching for my team and didn't see you." He dropped his drink and grasped the cyclist's arm, pulling her to a sitting position and looking for injuries. With his free hand, he brushed back masses of her dark hair. "I don't see any cuts."

She pushed his hand away. "I'm fine, considering I'm on my backside in the middle of a staging ground."

Good, she wasn't hurt. Sterling stood and pulled her upright. She appeared five years younger than he—twenty or so. Her tanned skin glistened golden in the sunlight.

"What did you do to my bike?" she gasped, and she kneeled beside the fallen cycle.

"If anything is damaged, I'll have it fixed." He helped her raise her bicycle upright, noticing the strength in her slender arms and the scent of peach shampoo from her hair. "Our team mechanic has everything."

"I have to race today." She frowned as she bent over the front wheel. "It's the only bike I have."

Sterling leaned forward to see how the spokes looked. The woman straightened and bumped into his chin, sending a sharp pain through his head.

She narrowed dark eyes as she rubbed the crown of her head in irritation. "Did Mary-Reva Brown send you over here?"

Sterling rubbed his chin and took a step back. "No, I—"

"It won't do any good. I'm going to win. You can't stop me."

Sterling threw back his shoulders and grinned. "You're accusing me of sabotage?"

Bolts of annoyance flashed as her gaze swept over him, but her expression just as quickly softened. Lines crinkled at the sides of the biggest brown eyes he'd ever seen. Her laughter tingled down his spine.

"No, a Silverwing wouldn't stoop to sabotage. Hard to believe clumsiness either." She shook her head and checked out the rear tire. "A Silverwing certainly shouldn't be so uncoordinated."

Glad for once to be recognized as a member of the top-rated men's pro team, Sterling grasped the ends of the towel that was draped around his neck. "You racing with a team?" He didn't recognize her colors, but she had mentioned Mary-Reva Brown, the lead cyclist on the Orange-Lite team.

"I'm on my own."

"The Orange-Lites are pros. Think you have what it takes to win over them?"

She tossed her hair over her shoulders and winked. "Watch and see."

What spunk. Sterling envied her enthusiasm. When was the last time he'd felt that way about a race?

"I saw the starting times," he said. He held her bike while she checked the chain. "The women's category isn't far behind the men's. You'll probably run into the lagging packs."

She straightened, a frown creasing her brow. "That could be a problem. You won't be there, will you?"

Sterling flattened a hand against his chest in mock protest. "I'll be up front."

She pointed to his Gatorade cup, on its side in a puddle next to her bike. "Don't forget your drink," she teased.

Sterling bent to pick up the cup, lifting the lid to see what remained, only to find that she was walking away. "Hey, wait up. What's your name?"

She paused and turned to face him, her gaze locking with his. Seconds ticked away, yet time seemed to stand still. An unfamiliar thrill coursed through Sterling.

He caught up to her and smiled. "I want to know the winner when her name is announced."

Her olive skin darkened with a blush. "Debra Valenzuela."

"Sterling Wade."

Before he could grasp her outstretched hand, someone bumped him from behind. His remaining Gatorade sloshed out of the now-open cup—and all over Debra Valenzuela's racing outfit.

She jumped, barely hanging on to her bike. "What else are you going to do to me?"

Sterling grabbed his towel from around his neck and started patting her dry. "What an idiot I am. Let me—"

Debra stepped back as far as she could and still maintain her grip on her bicycle. "What're you doing?"

"Trying to get you dry. You can't race with all that sticky—"

She pushed his hand away. "Who do you think you are? Some wacko version of Prince Charming?"

"I only wanted to help." Sterling forced himself not to laugh—or to visibly notice all the soft curves under the damp Lycra.

"You're not being any help at all." She turned her back to him and spoke over her shoulder. "On second thought, why don't you go 'help' the Orange-Lites."

Her chuckle mingled with the noise of the crowd as she pushed her bike into the throng.

Sterling remained rooted to the spot, unable to take his eyes off Debra Valenzuela until she'd vanished from sight.

His heart pounded. His fingers tingled. He laughed and shook his head. Too bad he couldn't get this excited about the race.

The male cyclists began to queue up at the starting line.

Tension. Excitement. Determination. Young blood. He could see it in the men. He saw it in Debra. Why didn't he have it anymore?

Maybe he was getting too old.

Wind whipped through Debra's helmet, tugging at loose strands of hair and cooling her off to a small degree. Adrenaline rushed through her system. Determined to win the race, she couldn't be in a better position as she pedaled down the Arizona highway. So why did such strange longings tug at her?

She gritted her teeth against the pain in her muscles and pedaled into the pack of lagging male cyclists, men who, for one reason or another, wouldn't have a prayer of winning their race.

Seconds later the road curved across the Arizona desert, and the crosswind hit from the left. Her wheels sang on the smooth pavement. Fifteen men were ranged in roughly two rows of bicycles, and Debra saw her chance to pass through the pack. Cacti dotting the desert floor became a blur as she sped past. Debra grabbed her water bottle to swallow some glucose for quick energy. The orange-flavored drink surged into her system. She lowered the plastic jug back into its cage.

It had been a gamble to break from the women behind her and bridge the gap into this bunch. If she could put these men between her and Mary-Reva, she would have a chance at the women's first place. It looked as if she just might pull it off.

Spurred on by the thought, Debra pushed aside the throbbing ache inside her. She had to win. *Papá.* She had to prove to him that she was as good as her brothers and sisters.

Debra powered behind another male cyclist. That couldn't be Wade, could it? Not this far back in the race. Muscles rippled as the man shifted position. She could see blond hair beneath the helmet and the angular chin she had bumped into earlier.

Good grief. Better steer clear of him, or she'd end up in a heap of mangled bicycle and bruised body parts.

Number Twenty cruised to her right. "Get lost," the cyclist growled as he edged closer. "Drop back with the other women, where you belong."

Debra briefly glared at the dark-haired man, then forged to her next position. She hadn't recognized his red jersey. *Must be an independent.*

Pain suddenly shot through Debra's right shoulder. She flinched and struggled to keep her balance. The malicious grin on Number Twenty's face told her he was the one who'd elbowed her.

"I said, move it." He reached out to strike again.

Debra dodged the blow, but she lost time with the sway of her bicycle. The Silverwing she thought might be Sterling Wade crossed in front and edged Number Twenty to the right side of the road.

"That's enough, Davis!" the Silverwing shouted. "Let her through."

"No dumb woman—" Davis started to protest, but the Silverwing closed in on him and forced him to back off.

Debra powered into the position the Silverwing had just vacated. She took in deep gulps of air, struggling against the wind and the possibility of another threat.

"I'll keep Davis off your back," the Silverwing said as he caught up to her. It *was* Sterling Wade.

Behind them, Davis let loose a string of curses aimed at Debra and her unexpected ally. "Ride with the women, Wade, but don't mess with me again."

"Glad you were there," she said, the closest to thanking him she could afford. She could be disqualified for accepting his help, and she didn't dare risk it.

"Providence." He smiled and leaned into the wind.

Providence, schmovidence. He should've been leagues ahead by now. Five-eleven and about twenty-five years old, Sterling Wade was not the number-one male racer, but his team, the Silverwings, was the best. That put him in the class of cyclists at the top.

He must've had mechanical problems, she decided. *Unless . . . No. Impossible.* He wouldn't *really* be out to sabotage her. If his goal was to disrupt her racing, he wouldn't have interfered with Davis.

Another curve loomed as the road climbed out of a ravine. Debra leaned forward, trying not to notice the man next to her yet unable to help herself. Sweat streaked down the chiseled cheek she could see. Muscles bunched in his powerful legs with each stroke of the pedals.

Debra forced herself to refocus on the road that cut through huge saguaro cacti standing like sentinels among red sandstone boulders.

The pack shifted again, and Debra pedaled hard.

She had to break through this group soon, or she'd be accused of drafting off the men. Debra couldn't afford that, not if she wanted to impress Mary-Reva and her team's manager, Hugh Ashford.

Wind whipped her cheeks as she rode into its force. She filled her lungs with deep breaths of dry desert air, air heavy with the pungent odor of sage. Precision timing, conditioned muscles, and months of training were finally paying off. This race was hers. She could taste victory.

That would give Mary-Reva and Ashford something to consider. Even though Debra biked for a small team, the Desert Roadrunners, that barely had funds to keep them in gas for their trips to the races, Ashford would definitely notice her if she won this race. Maybe he would invite her to join the Orange-Lites.

Tires singing, Debra pedaled into another curve. No one, not even her managers, Ralph and Cindy Robbins, knew she came from a dirt-poor family in a rustic town in central California but was determined to make it big, just as her brothers and sisters had done. They'd succeeded through their academic achievements. Debra had to find another way. And the Orange-Lites could be it.

Orange-Lite, a soft-drink company that supplied half the nation with a variety of beverages, sponsored a team that was good enough to race the circuit in Europe. That was Debra's goal, her dream.

Then *Papá* would be proud of her.

The thought of finally giving her father something to be proud of spurred her on. She took another drink of glucose and passed two more cyclists.

"Attack! Attack!"

The warning shout cut into Debra's concentration. Someone was trying to break through their ranks. Debra lowered her head and pummeled the pedals. Sterling Wade stayed close by. Should she be grateful or worried?

The pack stayed together. The attacker didn't make it.

Multiple gears clicked into place, and Debra shifted. The pack was slowing to catch their breath. Debra made her move and powered through the wind to the front. Ahead of the men.

Curses rang out behind her. She grinned. Those men would

now know a woman could keep up with them. Debra smiled in spite of the muscle burn in her legs and the frantic gulps of air that she took into tight lungs.

Now she had an edge. Mary-Reva would also have to get through the pack of cyclists to catch her. Would she leave the protection and support of her Orange-Lite teammates?

Debra cruised at high speed for a couple of miles until she saw the barn in the open field. The long climb was coming up. She grabbed the bottle of water and sprayed it across her head and shoulders. The liquid refreshed her hot body for mere seconds before evaporating.

The men would power past her on the steep climb, but downhill was her specialty. As long as she could stay ahead of Mary-Reva and the pack of women, she should have no problem passing through the men again. That would mean cycling by Sterling Wade.

Images of the Silverwing flashed across her mind. His smile. His silver-gray eyes. His sense of humor.

Stop thinking about him. Push on.

Her muscles burned in agony. She wanted to wipe the sweat from her brow.

No. Don't show any sign of weakness.

Her teeth ached with the effort of keeping her smile as she stood and threw her bike side to side to achieve maximum pull.

"What's she doing?" Davis yelled, his voice harsh.

"She's priming for the hill. Lay off."

Was that Wade? Sure enough, he inched slightly ahead.

Adrenaline mixed with panic.

No. Keep on smiling.

"Ease up, man. She'll drop back on this grade," someone behind her grunted.

"No way. Look at her. She's not even puffing."

Debra grinned. Just what she wanted them to believe.

"Pull, man. You're going to have to hustle for this one."

Several oaths echoed down the grade. Debra ignored the vise squeezing her lungs and focused on the hill ahead.

"Don't let a woman show you up."

"Yeah, man. Jump past her."

More cyclists passed, but Debra didn't worry. Their labored breathing told her what she wanted to know. These men were going to burn their reserves just to salve their pride. *Fine.* She'd catch up while they eased off to recuperate.

At the top she glanced back. Mary-Reva's pack was just beginning the climb. Debra streamlined her position and shifted to a lower gear. Alternately she braked and released to avoid overheating the wheel rims. The wind whistled through her helmet and whipped against her damp skin. By the time she reached the base of the hill, the men were forming another pace line. Debra broke into a sprint. She had to get past the men before the gate closed.

She watched the cyclists forming another echelon. She'd never get in if Number Twenty ended up as what the pros called "the ticket puncher at the gate," or the cyclist at the rear of the echelon. The person who had last place in the line had control of who came into the packs.

Debra's wheels sang. Her heart pounded. She had to win.

Chapter Two

Sterling glanced over his shoulder and saw the flash of kelly green closing in. A smile curved his lips in spite of the giant gulps of air he took in. Debra had made it. He'd thought she would. He'd positioned himself at the gate. For her.

She'd looked cool and collected when he'd passed her on that grade. Too cool. He had a feeling she was putting on a show to disconcert the guys. It had worked. He shook his head in admiration.

"Don't let her through, Wade!" someone shouted.

Probably the hotshot in the red jersey.

"What's the matter, Davis? Afraid of a little competition?" another cyclist ribbed.

The comments continued to rumble, but Sterling ignored them. His team was leagues ahead, hopefully in first place. Eddie Smith, the Silverwings' number one man, had had a flat tire. Sterling had pulled out and given Eddie his rear wheel. Smith had gone back into the race, losing only seconds, while Sterling waited for the support vehicle.

Sterling could easily move up to another position, but he didn't trust Davis. An odd sense of protectiveness kept him back and close to Debra.

The pace picked up with the threat of the woman joining in. Sterling eased over to make room. He heard her sharp breaths as she poured out her reserve.

Bright green flashed in the corner of his eye. He turned his head and gave her a nod. "Nice move. You'll get a short break in my draft."

She grinned.

What a looker. If she always flashed smiles like that, she'd get through without contest. Sterling shook his head at the thought.

Meters sped by as they moved in the pack. Sterling scarcely noticed the others as Debra Valenzuela followed close behind him. He'd never seen her before today. Who was her sponsor? Was she a local based here in Arizona?

The Phoenix metropolitan area attracted many cyclists. They could ride all winter long in the Sun Belt city. The growing population provided a market for multiple bike shops and probably just as many teams.

Sterling cycled out of a curve. Strange, though, most of the time women cyclists made a point of getting introduced to the Silverwings. Debra hadn't, and that interested him. Or had she? Could she have run into him on purpose? No. Her annoyance had been genuine. Too bad it wasn't a Sunday ride-along, or he'd ask about her sponsor.

For sure she wouldn't appreciate questions now. He recognized the look of someone hungry for a win. Didn't he used to have the same drive? From the determined set of her jaw and the smarts she'd shown so far, he guessed she'd capture the lead.

When his turn to point the echelon came up, he slowed the pace. Now she could make her break. Her gears clicked, and she leaned forward. *Good.* She'd recognized her chance.

Smart woman. Now, push.

Her muscles bunched and flowed, proving she was in shape to handle the rest of the race. Sterling wanted to see her finish.

"Get a move on, Wade!" Davis shouted. "You're slowing us down."

"Take a break, Davis. You need it."

Davis' tone turned derisive. "Against you?" he challenged. "Or a woman?"

Sterling didn't waste breath or emotion responding. What did it matter if they came in fiftieth instead of fortieth? Didn't Davis realize he'd already lost?

Debra had a chance to place first in the women's division. Before the race he'd favored Mary-Reva Brown to win, but he hadn't known about this one.

His turn to drop back in the echelon was coming up. Or he could move ahead. That had been his original plan, until Debra had joined the group; then he'd decided to stay behind and see how she fared. But she was on her way now. Time to make his own move.

His wheels spun with a low hum on the flat stretch of road. The desert scenery whizzed by his peripheral vision like a fast-forwarded movie.

He grinned. The lagging pack was turning out to be an interesting challenge. He'd love to see Debra come in ahead of Davis. He was a loudmouthed show-off, not to mention dangerous with his below-the-belt tactics. The man could use a lesson in humility.

Several miles passed, and Debra held her lead. A curve in the road was ahead. Now was his chance.

The change in wind direction gave him a push. In a flash of speed, Sterling shot forward. Puffing hard, he inched out of the pack and closed in on Debra. Her steadfast motion spurred him on.

The road straightened, and he pedaled beside her. His body blocked the wind that blew from the side. If he chatted for a minute, she'd have a breather. He shouldn't help the woman during a race, but who'd fault a guy for some friendly conversation?

"Who's your sponsor?" he asked, flashing a grin.

She picked up her pace to get out of his draft. "Don't interfere. You'll disqualify me."

With a burst of speed he powered beside her. "You should know who your friends are."

"You're a friend?"

"Your knight in shining armor. Prince Charming. Remember?"

She shook her head as she bent over the handlebars. "*Corny* is more like it."

"I did actually help out this time. Does that make up for earlier?"

Her laughter trailed behind her, making him think of things he had no business thinking about in the middle of a race. Maybe he was getting light-headed. He swigged some glucose and noticed she did too. She sent him a smile.

"Desert Cyclery," she finally replied. "They sponsor the Desert Roadrunners." She lowered her shoulders, ready to sprint again.

"Take it easy," Sterling assured her. "I'll be off in a second. I'll find you after the race."

Debra eyed the man beside her. The draft of wind he provided helped to restore her reserves, but it made her nervous. What if one of the cyclists—like that nasty Number Twenty—filed a complaint about Wade's giving assistance? Sterling Wade had helped her out of a tight spot back there. But surely no one would fault him. Not after the way she'd been fouled. She owed Wade. She could at least be friendly.

"Look for an orange VW van—says *Desert Cyclery* on it."

"Right." He saluted with two fingers to his helmet. Then he reached across, tapped her on the knee, and moved off.

It was a standard signal, but his light touch sent unexpected shivers through her.

Must be nerves. The end of the race neared.

The Silverwing zipped ahead. Debra admired Wade's skill. He leaned forward, minimizing wind resistance, and swerved smoothly around bumps in the road. The man knew how to ride.

She envied him his sleek machine. If she made it on to the Orange-Lite team, she'd splurge and get one like it. Her factory bicycle was top of the line, but a custom bike did wonders for speed and handling.

Dream away, she chided herself. But then again, wasn't that what *Papá* always insisted on? *"Dreams,* mi hija. *You got to have dreams, or you don't go nowhere. You stay here—in* barrio—*with nothing."*

Dreams she had plenty of, but she hadn't been given the brains to leave the *barrio* the way her brothers and sisters had. They'd finished college, gone on to have careers. She'd dropped out of the state university.

Thinking of her father spurred her on. She had to win this race. She had to get on to the Orange-Lite team. Or how would she face her father? She couldn't bear to disappoint him—again.

A commotion sounded from behind her. Shouts and jeers. Debra chanced a quick peek and almost fell off her bike. *Mary-Reva.*

Debra grunted in protest. Frustration and single-minded stubbornness were the only things keeping her going now. She refused to let Mary-Reva win. Not after all this hard work. Weeks of training. Countless hours of workouts and untold miles of cycling. Endless strategy sessions.

This race was hers. It had to be.

Buildings outlined the horizon. The cyclists were cruising out of the desert and back into town. It was mere meters to the finish. A flash of silver caught her eye up ahead. *Sterling.* He was closing in on another pack of men just entering town.

Seeing the Silverwing reminded Debra that she wasn't alone. Other Desert Roadrunners—the men—had raced ahead of her. Men who'd accepted her as the lone female on their team. They'd be at the finish, urging her to victory.

She leaned low on the handlebars. "Stay calm. Focus," she reminded herself.

Each breath filled her lungs with explosive agony. Blood rushed through her head and pounded in her ears. Debra ignored the screams of her system to stop this torture. Her whole body burned with pain.

"Go! Go! Go!"

Crowds lined the highway. Out of the corner of her eye she could see arms waving, people jumping up and down, shouting and screaming. That meant only one thing. Mary-Reva had to be close.

Debra didn't look. She refused to consider losing. She focused on the road ahead and pictured herself crossing the finish line first. Victory would be hers. She'd make it happen.

She saw the last corner. One block more and she'd be at the finish. Her grip tightened on the bars as she leaned into the curve. She whipped past buildings and then saw the flags. A time clock flashed minutes and seconds in big red letters as Debra flew across the finish.

She'd done it.

First place.

Blood rushed in her ears, blocking out the sounds of the crowd cheering as she sped past. She cried and laughed at the same time.

After two laps around the huge parking lot, Debra's system cooled down. She spotted her team's van and headed toward it. Ralph spun his wife, Cindy, around in circles. Tex and Red, her teammates, clapped each other on the back.

Her team. Celebrating victory. *Hers.*

So why did the odd yearnings persist? Shouldn't they have been assuaged by this win? She shook back her hair and breathed deeply, trying to shake off the strange longing.

On her way to the van, Debra searched the staging grounds for a sign of Sterling Wade. Splashes of silver appeared here and there, but none proved to be the lanky blond. Annoyed at herself for even looking, she cruised to a stop in front of her teammates and eagerly grabbed the Thirst Buster Cindy had in her hand.

"What happened to Mary-Reva?" Debra asked between gulps of the cool liquid that took away some of the coppery taste of stress from her mouth. "Why didn't she sprint ahead of me?"

"She'd gone the limit," Ralph told her as he handed her a towel. "She'd spent her last bit of energy catching up to you."

Debra took the towel and wiped away the perspiration still pouring down her face. "You saw what happened, then. That was miles out."

Ralph hadn't raced. He'd turned forty and gone from Senior to Veteran status last year and decided to drop out. Now he spent his time training Tex, Red, and her. Debra suspected he'd conceded to include a woman racer because of Cindy. The spunky blond insisted that featuring both sexes was good business for their cycle shop. Debra didn't care about the politics. She was just thankful for their sponsorship.

Ralph took her bike from her and leaned it against the van. "We drove to the hill outside of town and watched the last few miles with the binoculars."

Cindy took Debra's towel and bobbed her head. "I was praying like crazy. Who was the Silverwing?" Cindy added with a hint of teasing in her tone.

A curious excitement coursed through Debra as she explained her encounters with Sterling Wade. Her already heated cheeks flushed as she imagined *his* hands pressing the towel to her skin. Her breath caught as she remembered the strange electricity that had passed between them in those brief seconds they had shared.

Pushing aside her reaction to the Silverwing, Debra explained the problem with Number Twenty. "I don't know what would have happened if Sterling Wade hadn't been there."

Ralph bent his lanky form to inspect her bike. "Reporting a foul at this point isn't worth the hassle. You may come across him again in a later race."

"I wouldn't mind giving him a taste of my fist," Tex growled.

"Let's find the dude," Red joined in, his carrot-colored hair blowing in the wind.

Debra grabbed Red's arm before he headed off to find Davis. "Ralph's right. He was just mad because I passed him."

Cindy started laughing. "You know how it hurts the male ego to be beaten by us females."

"You got that right," Tex admitted with a sheepish grin. "You've had me worried a few times, girl."

Debra danced like a boxer around the two men, popping them with playful jabs to the shoulder. "Come on, you guys. You know I'm good. Admit the obvious."

Red rolled his eyes skyward. "Are you kidding? It's bad enough now, living with your swelled head."

Like a mother hen, Cindy stepped between Debra and her two teammates. "Give her a break. She just raced against the men, didn't she? Where'd *you* goof-offs place?"

Tex pretended to look aggrieved. "We didn't do so bad."

"Eleventh and twelfth places aren't peanuts, especially when Eddie Smith's racing." Red handed his bicycle to Ralph to be put away next.

Ralph hoisted the bicycle to the top of the van and fastened it onto the rack. "You all did fine. But don't get cocky. I saw plenty of room for improvement." He fixed a stare at Debra. "In all of you."

Debra took off her helmet. With a shake of her head, dark curls tumbled about her shoulders. "Don't tell me now. Let me have some glory. At least for a little while."

"Sure, Tiger." Red tousled her hair, an action she should've minded but didn't because it reminded her of her brothers. "Let's celebrate."

Cindy's hand shaded her eyes as she looked past them. "Don't leave yet. Someone's coming, and I bet he wants to see you, Debra."

Debra's heart raced. Her stomach tightened with instant nerves. Was Hugh Ashford coming to talk about the Orange-Lite team? *Please, please let it be him.*

When she turned around, Debra's heart sank and jumped at the same time.

Tall and dressed in silver, blond hair blowing in the wind, Sterling Wade strode toward her with confident strength.

Chapter Three

Debra struggled to hide her mixed feelings. To protect her in the pack, Sterling had subjected himself to ridicule from the other men. She was more than grateful. And something about the Silverwing made her breath catch and her heart skip a beat—sensations she didn't even want to acknowledge.

But right now she wished it was Hugh Ashford approaching to compliment her on her racing ability.

Sterling closed the gap between them, both arms raised high. "You did it. You gave those guys and Mary-Reva a run for their money."

"Thanks for your help," she said, taking a step back.

Sterling lowered his arms. "The least I could do, after our awkward meeting before the race."

Debra chuckled at the reminder but then frowned. "I just hope I don't get into any trouble because of your help."

"There were plenty of witnesses that Davis fouled you. He would be foolish to file a complaint." Sterling sent her a pleading grin. "Forget Davis. Celebrate. You just pulled off a coup. The Orange-Lites are tough to beat."

Debra relaxed. At least from worry. Her body zinged with new energy, something that seemed to happen regularly now around Sterling Wade. Something she dared not explore.

"Come meet my friends." She gestured him into the group. "Ralph and Cindy Robbins own Desert Cyclery. They're my sponsors."

Ralph extended his hand. "Sponsor, coach, trainer, mechanic. You name it—that's me."

"Jack-of-all-trades," Sterling commented as he shook hands.

Ralph took over the introductions. "These two are our senior cyclists. This here's Red Barnes. Meanest temper, if you can ever get him serious enough to lose it."

The blush that crept across Red's freckled face made Debra chuckle. Red was so easy to fluster, but he'd stand by you in a flash.

"And Tex here can sprint faster'n a jackrabbit once he sets his mind to it."

Sterling shook Tex's hand. "Nice one on the first stretch. You almost had Eddie Smith."

Tex shrugged as if it were nothing, but Debra knew the twenty-year-old was soaking in the praise. Another point for Sterling.

"And I guess you've already met our star." Ralph pointed to Debra as he draped an arm around his wife, Cindy. "She won't be with us Roadrunners for long. Wouldn't you say she's well on her way to a pro team?"

Heat crept up her neck. "Trying to get rid of me, Ralph?" Debra stepped toward Sterling and offered her hand to shake. "Thanks again for the help."

Strong fingers folded around hers and tightened when she tried to pull away. She gasped as tingles shot up her arm.

"It was worth losing a few places to see her beat out Davis," Sterling told the men, but he remained focused on Debra.

She looked straight into his eyes. Silver gray. They danced with friendly mischief.

Ralph dropped his arm from around Cindy's shoulders and moved next to Debra. "She told us what happened out there. Thanks for taking care of her."

Good ol' Ralph. Worse than her brothers, with the protective routine.

"No problem." Sterling winked and backed away, his fingers sliding away from hers, leaving an empty feeling. "Come meet the Silverwings," he invited. "We're always interested in up-and-coming cyclists."

Red and Tex fairly burst with eagerness to accept the offer. Debra had to admit she was tempted to join them, but she decided against going. If Hugh Ashford saw her busy with the Siverwing, he might not want to talk to her.

"You go on ahead. I've got things to do." She reluctantly waved them off. "You going, Cindy?"

Cindy shrugged. "Doesn't matter. Want your rubdown now?"

"Do you mind?" Debra asked hopefully.

Sterling reached over and lightly tugged a strand of her hair. "Sounds like you're avoiding me."

Debra chuckled and shook her head in denial. "I'd like to meet your team, but later. I have some things to take care of." *Like talk to Hugh Ashford.* "Besides, I need to clean up."

He shrugged and backed away. "We have a suite at the Cottonwoods Resort. Come by this evening. It's an open house. Friends drop in, and we rehash the race."

A suite. Must be nice. Debra couldn't help but think about the small room all five of them shared to cut down on costs whenever they were on the road. From the looks on their faces, the others were thinking along the same lines.

Ralph jumped in to accept. "Seeing your setup will give us something to aspire to."

That's Ralph. Always looking at things from the bright side. Personally, Debra would rather not let anyone know she was green with envy.

Sterling grinned. "It's a deal. Just ask at the desk for directions. In the meantime, why don't you guys come join us?" Sterling waved the men forward. "We'll leave the women to their business."

Red and Tex needed no more persuasion. They had already covered ten paces before Ralph even said good-bye to Cindy.

"Will I see you later?" Sterling asked Debra.

Debra debated. She should stay away from the Silverwing, yet it would be fun to experience firsthand a Silverwing party. "This evening," she agreed.

"Promise?"

She locked her gaze with his. Electricity hummed between them.

He smiled. A pleased smile that told her that he'd felt the same current.

Debra nodded. "Promise."

Sterling turned to follow Ralph. Debra tightened her hands into fists to keep them from reaching out to him. *Good grief. I'm acting like a silly groupie.*

She should be thinking of Hugh Ashford and the Orange-Lites, not a Silverwing—even an attractive Silverwing. Grinning, Debra watched Sterling as he headed toward the huge silver motorhome parked near the bandstand.

Once he was out of sight, she searched the crowd. The neon orange and hot pink jerseys of the Orange-Lite team should be easy to spot. But there were too many people milling about. All she could see was a jumble of heads and faces.

"Come lie down in the back of the van," Cindy called out.

Debra heard her friend rummaging around the crowded interior. "They'll be announcing the winners soon, so I'll just stay in my jersey."

Cindy popped out the door. "I got another Thirst Buster. You looked like you could use one."

That sounded like a good idea and tasted even better. The icy liquid soothed her throat and filled her dehydrated body. Debra drained the drink before she crawled into the back of the van.

"Just get my legs for now. They're starting to cramp."

Cindy pushed Debra onto the padded mat that took up nearly the whole floor. "Relax. You're still keyed up from that race."

Debra eased back on her elbows. "I sure hope Ashford liked my racing maneuvers. You think he'll be mad at me for beating Mary-Reva?"

"I doubt he's thrilled that you aced out his top racer." Cindy began working the tight muscles of Debra's legs.

Debra flinched at the pain that shot through her with each push and prod. Cindy worked magic with her hands. She'd had a lot of practice during the years Ralph had raced.

"But if he knows I can beat her, wouldn't he want me on the team?"

"Don't get impatient. You know what Ralph says. You're going to have to race this whole season on your own." Cindy's fingers pressed into knotted flesh. "Make a name for yourself first. Get several wins under your belt."

Debra grimaced. "I hate waiting. I want it all *now.*"

"Patience has never been your virtue," Cindy agreed. "Why do you want to be on a pro team so badly? I know it's not the glory. You hate getting up in front of crowds."

"It is the glory in a way. I mean, if you have a name, you can pick your team." Debra rolled over, reached for a pillow, and lowered herself onto her back. Scents assailed her nostrils—the aroma of the almond lotion in contrast to the smell of the rubber bicycle tires, gear lubricants, metal tools, and sweaty socks and shirts cluttering the back of the van.

"Is it the money? I know we don't help much, but soon Ralph and I will have our business established, and we can provide more—"

"No, no," Debra hastened to reassure Cindy. "I love being on this team, but I want to do the circuit in Europe."

"Does it bother you that you're the only woman in the Roadrunners?" Cindy adjusted to Debra's new position and kneeled on the floor of the van.

"No. That's a plus for me. I have to push that much harder to keep up with the guys."

Debra had been on another Phoenix team that included over a hundred members. She'd been forced to ride with the other women, and they hadn't provided enough competition to give her an edge.

"Don't worry about the cash. My relatives back me financially," Debra assured her. "Besides, money doesn't begin to count against what you and Ralph do for my morale. I need your support."

"Ralph misses racing," Cindy confessed, as she pressed on more stiff muscles. "That's why he gives so much to you, Tex, and Red."

Debra had figured that, but she didn't really know what to say. Instead, she closed her eyes and focused on relaxing her aching muscles. Cindy's fingers kneaded and pulled at the stubborn knots, sending shots of pain followed by incredible relief through her weary legs.

Getting accepted on to a pro team would ultimately be a reward for Ralph and Cindy too. Their names would be linked to hers on the road to fame, which would attract cyclists to their team and the shop. The publicity and hype would be easier for her to face if her friends were benefiting from it. Personally, she disliked the glory game. She would be content just to ride her bicycle anonymously. But that wouldn't be enough to satisfy her father.

Debra rolled over onto her stomach so Cindy could get the back side of her long legs. She tucked her chin into the crook of one arm and dreamed of wearing the neon orange and hot pink colors of the Orange-Lite team. She imagined standing on the dais receiving a trophy and smiling as her win was televised in several languages to all the cities of Europe. *Papá* would be there too. Proud and beaming, as he'd been when her brothers and sisters received their diplomas.

Debra had tried higher education, but clearly she wasn't cut out for it. Not like her brothers and sisters. Reading was difficult for her and studying impossible.

It isn't fair. Debra moaned.

"Am I hurting you?" Cindy's question broke the silence of Debra's memories.

"No. Just thinking," Debra admitted, while she stretched her toes forward. "When you're finished, I think I'll go look for Ashford."

"Let him come to you. You'd be better off going to see Sterling Wade and the Silverwings."

"Why?"

"To impress Ashford with the company you keep."

The idea seemed distasteful, although seeing Sterling appealed.

"It doesn't hurt to have contacts," Cindy went on to explain. "Sterling Wade. Isn't he yummy?" She sighed, as she pushed and poked at Debra's calf muscles.

Debra flinched at the added pressure. "Not bad." Wade definitely had sex appeal, along with a sense of honor and a caring smile.

"It's not every day you meet a guy like that, and he definitely made it known that he's interested in you," Cindy pointed out.

"You know I don't have time for involvement now," Debra protested. She should feel indifferent, but his flirting had pleased her. *Odd.* She was usually immune, especially while racing. It must've been the high she'd gotten off her win.

"You need to date more." Cindy rambled on with the familiar theme. Debra half listened while sounds of other cyclists milling about outside the van divided her attention. "I mean, you spend every spare moment either working out or riding. You've got to have some fun in your life."

"Riding *is* fun," Debra insisted. "Sure, it would be great to kick back and take in a few of life's pleasures, but I have to accomplish my goals first." She couldn't bear to see any more tears in *Mamá*'s eyes. She refused to continue to put her brothers and sisters on the spot with her father's anger because they financed and defended her. No. She had to do this.

"You're a beautiful woman," Cindy said. "I mean, look at that hair. And your figure is perfect."

How many times had she fought off unpleasant advances while in junior high and high school? In the *barrio* Debra had learned the hard way that her beauty was best kept hidden under the guise of a rough tomboy exterior. "That isn't always an asset."

Cindy slapped Debra on the back, her way of saying she was finished. "Don't knock the looks," she advised. "They're a gift."

Debra scooted to the edge of the van and dropped her legs over the back bumper. She glanced with genuine envy at the older woman standing just outside. Cindy and Ralph shared a deep love and a faith that brought them through the tough times. Faith was something Debra didn't have much of, and she often wondered if it really made a big difference in one's happiness. Cindy and Ralph claimed it did.

Cindy climbed up into the van and started putting the equipment away. "You're going to be famous someday. You'll be in the spotlight."

"Not because of my looks," Debra reminded her. "Because of hard work and stubborn determination."

"But your looks will help." Cindy tossed towels aside as she glanced out at the crowd of cyclists and fans milling about. "You get a lot of attention from men. Use it to meet the right ones."

"You mean flirt with Hugh Ashford to get him to notice me?" Debra couldn't believe she was hearing that from Cindy. "Would that be ethical?"

"Why not?"

"Because I don't know how to flirt for real, let alone like that." Debra scooted off the bumper and turned around toward Cindy. "I've always been just one of the guys. I don't think I'd know what to say."

Cindy chuckled. "You don't have to say much of anything. Just smile a lot."

Debra shook her head, sending waves of dark hair across her shoulders. "Forget it. Given my history with the opposite sex, flirting would do me more harm than good."

Cindy grinned. "You just haven't met the right one yet. When you fall, I bet love hits hard."

"I hope not," Debra declared, more to assure herself than Cindy. "At least not until after I make it to Europe."

That morning she'd caught a few glimpses of Hugh Ashford. He was tall and built like a football player, with broad shoulders and thick thighs. She didn't care for a man towering above her. She preferred men who were lean and fit and more her size. *Someone more like . . . Sterling Wade? No, no, no.* She tossed the thought aside and turned back to Cindy.

"It's almost time to announce the winners. We should head that way." Debra pointed toward the bandstand, where a crowd was beginning to form.

Chapter Four

Sterling stood outside the thirty-foot recreational vehicle. He'd picked the Airstream more for the aluminum siding than for the fact that it was the Cadillac of motorhomes. The shiny silver went well with both the image and the logo of the Silverwings emblazoned on the sides of the vehicle. He leaned against the motorhome, absorbing the coolness from the metal.

Debra Valenzuela. He couldn't get her out of his mind. He'd felt an attraction. She had too. Was that mutual interest capturing his concentration, or was it the challenge she presented? Because he had also sensed her purposely pulling away from him.

Sounds from the staging grounds clamored for his attention. Noise that normally he could block out, but not today. A man nearby yelled at another cyclist. Tools clattered when tossed onto the cement parking lot. Sunlight reflected off equipment scattered throughout the staging area. Cyclists came and went.

Restless and edgy, Sterling listened to the voices around him.

"Did you see how that woman moved up through three packs of men?"

"I couldn't believe it. When she whizzed past me, I thought maybe I'd suddenly lost it. I mean, I move fast, but that one flew right by me."

It had to be Debra they were talking about. Sterling's interest in the conversation picked up.

"She's fast, all right. She trains with us, and, believe me, the challenge keeps us going," Red Barnes boasted as he shook his head.

Tex stepped over to his cycling buddy. "Red hates it when she gets by him."

"So do you, brother, so don't give me no flak."

The other men crowding around laughed.

"She trains with you guys, huh?" Eddie Smith asked. "So what are her plans? She's going to try for the Nationals, isn't she?"

Sterling moved away from the RV to get closer. He wanted to learn everything he could about Debra, and not only because of her cycling ability. When she'd smiled and flashed those dark eyes at him, he knew something special had passed between the two of them.

"Course she'll race the Nationals if she wins this season, but she's more interested in pro."

"Has her heart set on racing the circuit in Europe," Tex added.

Eddie whistled. "That's a tough circuit."

"She is tough," Red assured them. "I've never seen anyone with the drive that woman has."

"She'll need it."

Sterling agreed. The Silverwings had a team that raced internationally. He'd done the circuit once, when he was eighteen and a hotshot full of himself. Serious business in Europe, cycling was the second biggest sport after soccer. The teams and the public took the races to heart.

The conversation turned to discussing the race. Eddie started whining about his flat tire, and Sterling eased away. Lately the camaraderie of the team hadn't been enough for him. He worked hard all year so he could get time off to race during the season. Normally he loved rapping with the guys, being part of the team. But this year something was missing. He needed a new goal—a new challenge.

He glanced over at the orange VW van where he'd left Debra. What he really wanted was to go back and talk to her. He thought of the lithe brunet, standing there so relaxed and sure of herself, the breeze tossing her hair about her shoulders.

"Hey, Wade!"

The shout interrupted his fantasizing. Their team manager, Joe Carson, was yelling from the motorhome.

"Your dad is on the line."

Sterling started toward the door. "Probably wants to know how we placed."

"I already told him Eddie won."

Sterling groaned inwardly but kept the smile on his face. If Michael David Wade still wanted to talk to him, it could mean only one thing. Business.

"I'll round up the others and head them toward the bandstand," Joe said, as Sterling stepped inside the motorhome. "We should all be there when they hand out the prizes."

Joe left the Airstream. After making sure no one else was inside, Sterling locked the door. The team knew that Sterling and his father made up the partners who owned Coronado Industries, whose holdings included Silverwings, Inc. But they didn't know Sterling was the chief CEO during the winter months when the racing circuit was off-season.

Sterling worked his way to the front of the motorhome and picked up the phone. "Must be serious."

"You're going to have to come home, son. We've got a problem with the corporate division."

"I can get a flight into San Diego tomorrow morning. Will that be soon enough?" He hoped so. He didn't want to miss out on the opportunity to talk to Debra that evening.

"The board meeting's at ten, so get here in time to be briefed."

The board? It had to be critical if they were being called in. "Imperial Industries trying to steal our market again?"

"No. Someone's selling stock. A big percentage. Looks like a power play."

"I'll come straight to the office from the airport."

"I know I owe you some time. I need you, though, and this situation is also going to need some prayer."

"Count on it, Dad."

Sterling sighed as he hung up the phone. Running a big

business was a lot of work. It had held much excitement and satisfaction at one time. But lately it seemed like a chore. He wouldn't dream of giving it up, though. That would mean no more sponsoring teams on the racing circuit. Coronado Industries provided the biggest money offered to pros in the United States—salaries to the cyclists, professional managers and coaches, and all traveling expenses for both their international and national teams.

Coronado Industries also financed several inner-city programs for teens. They provided buildings and salaries for clergy and professional counselors. No way could Sterling or his father cut so many dedicated workers and young people out of jobs or support.

What he really needed was a new challenge. He had established a winning pro team, headed a large corporation, and become a successful cyclist. Now, however, he felt he had no meaningful purpose. No new goals. No focus.

Sterling made his way to the refrigerator, located in the back of the motorhome, and grabbed a bottled water. As soon as he'd received his MA degree, his father had brought him in as a partner in the family business, and they'd worked out a deal. Sterling managed the business during the winter months while his dad golfed and helped organize fund-raisers for several of his pet causes.

The senior Wade took over during the spring and summer while Sterling dropped his corporate image and became a professional cyclist. Usually the arrangement worked, except at times like this when an emergency surfaced.

Sterling downed the last of the water and walked outside. The dry air and bright sunshine warmed his skin. He searched the staging ground until he spotted a flash of kelly green.

Debra. She stood near the bandstand. The day suddenly seemed brighter, his step more alive. Now, there was something he didn't have in his life—a woman. His parents had been urging him to settle down, marry, start a family, but he hadn't been interested in tying himself down. The sight of Debra Valenzuela stirred longings that perhaps he should explore.

Eddie waved when he spotted Sterling. "They're about to announce the winners for the Women's Category."

Sterling hurried to catch up to his teammate.

The two Silverwings barely made it through the crowd to the bandstand in time for the announcement of the Junior Category's winners. They announced the Women's Category next, so he missed his chance to talk to the new star. He kept his eye on her, though.

Her dark hair was tossed about in the breeze. Eyes bright with excitement, she glanced out at the crowd and saw him. She smiled, and what a smile. He was definitely going to have to get to know her.

"She sure is a looker," Eddie commented when Debra accepted her cash prize, looking uncomfortable with the applause.

Sterling nodded, wondering if the spotlight embarrassed her. Her cheeks reddened as she nervously toyed with the envelope.

The announcements finally over, Sterling watched Debra leave the stage. The Silverwings had wrapped up first, second, and third in the Senior Men's Category, but he barely paid the wins any mind. He was too busy admiring the star female cyclist.

After all the winners were announced, the crowd began to disperse. Sterling tried to keep his eye on Debra, but he lost track of her in the throng. What direction had she taken?

Cyclists and fans milled around the parking lot of the shopping center, forming a kaleidoscope of color and sound. Smoke billowed from a nearby grill, tempting onlookers with the aroma of savory barbeque sauce and ribs. Helmets glistened in the bright sun as cyclists pedaled among the throng. Laughter highlighted the cacophony of voices.

Sterling wove his way through the crowd, peering over heads and glancing in every direction. What if she'd left already? He kept his eye on the orange van. It was still there. Good.

He finally found her, and he wasn't surprised to see who was standing beside her. Sterling eased past several people as he worked his way to the refreshment booth where Debra was talking to Mary-Reva Brown and her team manager.

Debra smiled at Hugh Ashford and Mary-Reva, hoping her efforts to be social were working. The Orange-Lite manager was at least listening to what she had to say.

"Will you be racing the circuit or just the local races?" Ashford asked.

"As many as I can," Debra assured him, her grip tightening on the envelope with the cash prize. "My boss at the store is pretty flexible."

"It'll be interesting to see how you do." He glanced at Mary-Reva.

The blond cyclist nodded.

"If you continue to do as well as you did today, we might want to talk," Hugh continued.

Excitement surged through her. Tempted to jump up and down, she worked to contain her composure. *Act calm,* she ordered her trembling body. This was it. He'd as much as said he'd be watching her.

A movement out of the corner of her eye caught her attention. A flash of silver. Before she knew what was happening, a strong hand grabbed her empty one.

"Congratulations! Nice win."

Laughing eyes captured hers. Sterling.

The world started to spin. She clutched her envelope with one hand and his with the other, too surprised to resist. The shock lasted for a second before reaction set in. She laughed. "In spite of your 'help.' "

"Must've been the Gatorade bath." Sterling chuckled as he shook her hand.

A mock frown creased her brow. "Or good old-fashioned skill."

"Guts and stamina," he agreed.

"It could have been luck." A male voice intruded.

Debra started. *Ashford and Mary-Reva.* Heat flushed her neck and face. She pulled away from Sterling. What would the Orange-Lite team manager think?

Sterling stiffened as he slowly released her hand. His face sobered, but his eyes were still smiling.

She struggled to regain her equilibrium. The crowd milling about came back into focus. The aroma of barbecue mingled with the smells of heated bodies passing nearby. Sunshine reflected off sunglasses and bicycle parts.

Taking a deep breath of the unseasonably warm March air, she grasped the prize envelope tighter and looked at her companions. Before she could apologize to Ashford and Mary-Reva, Sterling began talking.

"You going to let the Orange-Lites come to the party to-night?" he asked the team manager.

Ashford winked at Mary-Reva. "Miss a Silverwing bash, Wade? My team would never forgive me if we didn't go."

Sterling shoved his dark glasses to the top of his head, ignoring the tangle of blond hair. "And you won't let them out of your sight."

Ashford nodded in agreement.

To Debra's surprise, the two men talked as if they had known each other for years. They probably had; after all, they were both pros. Yet she sensed a reserve, especially on Sterling's part.

Sterling turned toward Debra and brought her into the conversation. "You've met the star, I see. Quite an upset. No offense, Mary-Reva."

Mary-Reva glanced at the prize envelope and then smiled at the Silverwing. "None taken, especially from you."

Debra observed the interchange between the two cyclists. Mary-Reva made it obvious that she was interested in the Silverwing. Maybe that was a good thing. Then Debra could have more of Ashford's attention.

Mary-Reva switched her focus from Sterling to her. "You're the toughest competition I've come up against."

Debra took a step away from Sterling and moved closer to Ashford. "I had a lucky break, that's all." She smoothed her palm over the edge of the envelope, the feel reminding her of the thrill of victory but also of the strange yearnings that had not disappeared with the accomplishment.

Sterling eyed her retreat. "I watched you pull up that hill. You've got a lot of drive and power."

The praise embarrassed Debra, yet the comments, clearly directed at Ashford, could only be helping. Did Sterling know what he was doing?

A quick glance at his face assured her that he did. But why would he go out of his way to promote her to the Orange-Lite manager? And why did his doing so make her edgy?

As if he sensed her uneasiness, Ashford backed away. "We've got to round up the team. Congratulations again." He smiled at Debra. "See you tonight."

Before she could respond, Sterling grasped her elbow and guided her away from the pair.

"You aren't going to disappoint him, are you?"

Debra pulled her arm free. "Why do I get the feeling you're maneuvering me?"

His smile had returned to his eyes. "Would I do that?"

She stopped and, shifting the envelope, fisted her hands on her hips. "You made sure I'd come to your party. To see Hugh Ashford."

"And that's a bad thing because . . . ?" He lifted both hands.

"Look, I appreciate your efforts, but I can manage on my own."

He cast her a look of mock dismay. "You mean I can't be your knight in shining armor?"

She chuckled. "Am I in need of one?"

He bowed. "Glad to be of service."

"Oh, brother." She groaned and started walking away from him.

He fell in beside her as she threaded her way through the

crowd toward her team's van. "If you're looking to get a shot at the Orange-Lite team, you'll need more than your cycling ability. Hugh's tough. Some inside contacts wouldn't hurt."

"Meaning you?" Debra stopped. Sterling bumped into her, sending a jolt through her system. "Look, I appreciate all you've done for me today."

"Why do I hear a *but* coming?" He tucked a strand of hair behind her ear.

She resisted the urge to grab his hand and looked straight into his gray eyes. "I really do want to get on the Orange-Lite team. And they have strict rules about relationships during racing season. I don't want Ashford to get the wrong idea."

His face sobered; his expression grew serious. "Come to the party to relax and enjoy yourself. He can't fault you for that."

Debra shrugged. "I usually make it a practice to stay away from parties." She'd seen many a good cyclist come down on performance after a night out with the fans and sponsors who supported the events.

"Nothing to be uptight about. We don't offer any alcohol. No drugs." He grasped her elbow and guided her out of the path of an oncoming cyclist. "We're in training too, remember."

True. The Silverwings did have a reputation for staying clean, which was why the Orange-Lites would be there. Debra chewed on her lower lip for a moment while she tried to sort out her emotions. "I suppose getting to know Ashford and the team on a social basis would be a good idea," she mused aloud.

"Of course." She thought she detected a hint of annoyance in his voice, but he continued. "Never hurts to network with the pros. It helps when you're out on the road to know who your friends are."

"Like today?" She cast him a smile. "I hope Number Twenty won't be at your party. I'm liable to give him a piece of my mind."

"At least we agree on that point." He chuckled. "We didn't invite him."

Before Debra could respond, she saw Cindy and Ralph waving from the van. Debra held up her fingers in a *V*, letting her sponsors enjoy the victory also.

"I'd better let you celebrate with your team." Sterling sounded reluctant.

"Yours won in the Senior Category. Surely you're going to cheer them on too."

"You've got a point." He waved her off. "Am I going to see you this evening?"

Debra nodded. She couldn't help but smile in response to the pleased expression on Sterling's face. Shaking her head, she threaded her way toward Cindy and Ralph.

Chapter Five

Ralph whisked the envelope of cash out of her hands and danced a jig around the van. Debra laughed, enjoying the sight.

Cindy grasped Debra's shoulders. "Wow! Not only did you bag the prize, but you hobnobbed with Ashford, Mary-Reva, and a Silverwing."

"Calm down. It wasn't that big of a thing." Yet she couldn't still her own nerves when she told Ralph and Cindy what Ashford had said.

Ralph shook his head. "I'm happy for you, Debra, but we'll sure hate to lose you to the Orange-Lites."

Debra brushed back her hair. "Please. I'm a long way from that. We have this season to get through first."

"And I'm going to enjoy using the time to make a champion out of you."

Debra returned Ralph's hug, thankful for his generous nature. "Besides, when I go national, I'm going to need a coach for the off-season. I'm hoping I'll be able to talk you two into it."

"You got it." Ralph laughed. "Where are Tex and Red? I'm ready to leave."

As if on cue, Debra spotted the two cyclists heading toward the van. Debra looked at her prize money and sighed, suddenly tired. The day had been grueling. A shiver of longing coursed through her, and again she wondered why the victory had not eased its intensity. This internal craving—maybe it wasn't for victory. But with victory she might finally have her father's respect. Surely that was what was still missing.

Debra straightened. A soak in the tub and a nap would be

perfect just now. She would call home, and then she'd see how she felt about going to the party. And about seeing Sterling Wade.

Debra couldn't stop staring at the plush accommodations of the Silverwings' suite. The size alone made the Roadrunners' usual small room shrink even more by comparison. In spite of the spaciousness, the suite was crowded.

"Can you believe this place?" Cindy commented as they were escorted inside.

Ralph took her sweater and handed it to someone handling wraps. The late winter days in the desert were warm, but the evenings turned chilly. "Take note. Someday we'll be staying in one of these suites."

Cindy spun around, taking in the sight of the vaulted ceiling, the fireplace, the built-in bar, and the view of Camelback Mountain. French doors opened onto a private patio and Jacuzzi.

Debra smiled. *Hard work. Determination.* That's how goals were accomplished. And the Desert Roadrunners had plenty of that.

Debra straightened the blue-jean vest she wore over her white blouse. "I recognize most of the people here. Looks like the whole racing circuit has moved into this suite."

Ralph waved at someone he knew. "I don't know about you two, but I'm ready for some refreshments."

Cindy pointed toward a complete dining room and kitchen area stocked with serving dishes of food. From the looks of the spread, the Silverwings knew what hungry cyclists wanted to eat.

Several plates held raw vegetables and creamy dressings. Others offered beautiful arrays of fruit. Baskets of rolls bordered cheese and meat platters.

At the bar, one of the team managers handed out bottles of fruit juice and spring water. Ralph went to get them something to drink. Debra scanned the room, looking for Sterling while she waited with Cindy.

"This is going to be great," Cindy commented. "You aren't too tired, are you?"

"No. That nap picked me right up." Fortunately, that afternoon she'd been able to take her bath right away and then crash. But it wasn't the rest that had inspired her to come to the party. She searched again for a sign of blond hair and gray eyes and chastised herself for doing so.

"I don't see how you can sleep with all the racket that goes on at your place, especially on the weekends."

Debra smiled. "The advantage of growing up with lots of brothers and sisters."

If Cindy only knew, she thought. The noise at the small house she now shared with three college students was mild compared to a day in the life of the Valenzuela family. Thinking of her family reminded her of why she was here. The phone conversation with her father earlier had not gone well.

"I won today, Papá. I beat out one of the top US teams."

"And I am supposed to be thrilled? Mi hija, you got to stop playing around. You aren't getting any younger."

She'd rolled her eyes and grasped the phone receiver until her knuckles turned white.

"You better come home. If you don't go to school, maybe you marry one of Alejandro's sons."

As if that will ever happen. She knew the Rodriguez boys well. Too well. They were like brothers.

Her father's next words had cut into her thoughts. *"They do well. Make lots of money."*

"I don't need anyone to support me." That wasn't entirely true. *"I'm going to make it big. You'll see."*

She would make it on her own. She'd show her family that she had what it took.

Debra shook off the memory and leaned over to Cindy. "I hope I get a chance to talk to Ashford tonight," she whispered.

Cindy nudged her arm and nodded toward the largest room. "Looks like your wish is granted."

Hugh Ashford had spotted her and was heading in her direction. Debra's heart raced. She glanced around for Sterling and again scolded herself for doing so.

Stick to business.

Cindy whispered, "Remember what I said earlier. It won't hurt to use your charm."

Debra stepped away, casting Cindy a look of dismay. Couldn't she make the Orange-Lite team on her cycling ability alone? Sterling had advised her to socialize with the team. Cindy wanted her to network with the manager. All she wanted was to get a chance to cycle with the elite.

Sterling knew that Debra Valenzuela had arrived the minute she stepped inside the suite. He sensed her presence, and one glance through the door of his bedroom toward the entryway had assured him she was there. The sight pleased him more than he would have thought possible. Too bad he couldn't break away from this impromptu meeting with his team and manager to go talk to her.

"What do you think of the idea, Wade?" Eddie Smith's question brought his attention back to the group.

"That's good for me. You go ahead and drive the Airstream to Tucson. I'll fly there in time to catch the next race."

The meeting dragged on. Restless and eager to leave, Sterling remained silent, praying for a quick end to the discussion. He wanted to find Debra before she became entangled in other conversations. Eddie laughed. Sterling had no idea what had been said, but he took advantage of the laughter to glance over at Debra. She'd stepped out of his range of vision. Quietly he edged toward the door.

She hadn't gone far; she stood glancing around the huge living room. Sterling liked her self-assured stance and the way she smiled at those around her.

Eddie nudged Sterling's shoulder. "What's up, Wade? Today's women's class winner got your interest, ol' buddy?"

He guided Smith away from the door. "As a matter of fact, yes. So take note, and stay clear."

Eddie nodded toward the other side of the suite. "Better get the word out. Hugh Ashford's on his way over. Don't let him near a female you want."

Sterling merely grunted his acknowledgment. He'd heard enough talk on the circuit to know that Hugh Ashford took advantage of the young women who wanted a position on the Orange-Lite team.

He pushed past Eddie. "Make way. I'm off to the rescue."

Behind him he heard the laughter of his teammates. There had been a time when he would have taken steps to avoid the ribbing he'd get now. But it didn't seem to matter anymore. More important issues were at stake here. Namely, Debra's well-being.

"Hey, Wade. Tough break out there."

"Too bad about your wheel."

The comments slowed him down as he wound his way through the crowd. One of the disadvantages of being on a popular team—you couldn't call your time your own, especially at a party that included the whole racing crowd.

"What happened on the hill climb?"

"Did you see the road rash on Jones?"

Sterling answered as quickly as he could and moved on without appearing too rude. He knew he didn't have to do much to carry a conversation. After a race everyone was eager to rehash the day's events.

"What about the upset to the Orange-Lites? Did Mary-Reva Brown get burned or what?"

At least the topic of this conversation interested him. "Debra Valenzuela. From a local team. Shows lots of promise, wouldn't you say?" he asked, before stepping around the group of women.

"Hold on there, Silverwing. We aren't going to let you get away that easily."

Too late he saw his mistake. *Martha Rogers.* Sterling groaned. His luck to run into one of the Silverwings' more aggressive groupies.

"How's it going, Martha? Glad you could make it to the meet."

She made every meet. He didn't approve of her constant

flirting, but he could never bring himself to be mean to her. She appeared lonesome and fragile in spite of her outward toughness.

Martha smiled and clasped her hands over her heart. "You always are the gallant one."

Restless to move on, Sterling glanced again in Debra's direction and edged around the woman. The Desert Roadrunner cyclist wouldn't be flattering and coy just because he was a Silverwing, and that pleased him. Some of the guys got off on the attention, but not Sterling. It seemed phony and a facade.

Debra's smile, on the other hand, was genuine. The fact that it was directed at Ashford instead of him was more disconcerting than he wanted to admit.

"Got some business to take care of, Martha. Make yourself at home," he offered as he pulled away.

Her gasp of protest barely registered as he moved farther into the crowded room. The closer he got to his goal, the slower his progress seemed to be.

A teammate slapped him on the back. "Wade, come here and tell this novice the facts."

Sterling inwardly groaned. Another delay. Feigning interest, he managed a smile.

"What's up?" he asked.

"I've been telling him that Campy is the only brand of tools to have. He thinks his brand is going to get him through the season."

"Campagnola's are the best." Sterling couldn't help but chuckle at the boy's rapt attention.

The seriousness of youth, he sighed inaudibly. Maybe he was getting too old for this. How long had it been since he'd had that awed enthusiasm?

A movement out of the corner of his eye caught his attention. He looked up and saw Debra cast him a quick smile.

Or maybe his interests were heading down new channels. Slowly Sterling worked his way from his teammates and closer to Debra, wondering why he was so determined to reach her.

He'd been perfectly happy with his bachelor life. He didn't need it complicated with a woman. Hadn't he always espoused the theory that serious cyclists needed freedom?

The racing circuit left little time for a relationship. There were hours of practice and workouts seven days a week. Each weekend in a different town. Constant travel made dating difficult, let alone granting time to form any lasting bonds.

He had been wise to remain detached from the opposite sex. At least during the racing season. True, he had more time during the winter when he was handling Coronado Industries. Yet even then he spent most of his spare time cycling.

Maybe he needed to change his habits. He wanted to talk to Debra, and he had almost reached her.

"I'd like to see you work out," Ashford commented, as he took a step closer to Debra. "Maybe tomorrow before we leave town."

Debra backed up toward Sterling. "That could be arranged. I'm sure Ralph can pick me up early."

Sterling didn't waste a moment. "Hi, Debra. Sounds like you need a ride. I'm available."

The moment the words were out, Sterling knew he was in trouble. First off, he'd forgotten about flying to San Diego. Second, Debra did not look at all pleased with his offer.

Debra couldn't believe Sterling Wade had interfered again. Why did he have to show up every time she was talking to Hugh Ashford? And why did she have to be so pleased that he had?

"No need. Ralph will want to be there."

Not only that, she needed Ralph to help set her paces. Sterling looked slightly relieved. Surely he didn't feel obligated to offer just because he had knocked her down earlier that day, did he?

Ashford extended his hand to her. "It's a date, then. We'll see you in the morning."

"Deal." She shook his hand.

As soon as the Orange-Lite manager left, Debra swung around to face Sterling.

"There's no need for you to feel responsible for me."

"Your knight, at your service, remember?"

She ignored his reminder, and the smile went out of his gray eyes.

"It's wise to be a little careful around Hugh Ashford," he said seriously.

"Thanks for the tip, but I want to encourage all the contacts I can." She frowned slightly. "Isn't that what you advised me to do, socialize with him?"

Sterling shifted from one foot to the other. "On a professional basis."

"Then what's wrong with my meeting him tomorrow? Ralph will be there."

Sterling's frown eased some but not the seriousness in his expression. "You're new to the pro circuit. Some men take advantage of inexperienced women, especially beautiful ones."

"And Hugh Ashford is one of those men?"

Sterling didn't say anything. At least he had enough conscience not to spread gossip. Surely she'd already heard about Ashford. Everybody had.

She cut a glance at Sterling. "I've also heard about you. Maybe I shouldn't be talking to you either, huh?"

"Caution never hurts. Though I can assure you, my intentions are only for your protection."

Actually, the word on Sterling Wade had never been nasty. He wasn't known to pick up women on the circuit—not cyclists or fans. Some suspected he had a woman at home. Debra didn't pay much heed to rumors. She liked to make her own judgments.

"Is there someone back home?" she asked bluntly.

He smiled again and shook his head. "No, haven't had time to devote to a relationship."

Relief flooded Debra, and she mentally kicked herself for it. "Not even occasional encounters on the road?"

"Especially not those." His eyes locked with hers. Sincerity glinted in their depths. "I've never been one to indulge in casual relationships. Goes against my values."

Debra couldn't help but smile back before she broke eye contact. "Well, then, we have that in common—the values part, anyway."

Promiscuity was strictly against her morals. And she'd suffered dearly for her abstinence in high school and college.

"That shows wisdom on your part."

His response surprised her. How refreshing to be able to talk frankly with a guy and not have to fend off the usual come-ons. If she was completely honest with Sterling, she'd have to admit that Hugh Ashford *had* made insinuations along with shoptalk. She'd fended them off as she always did.

Sterling placed a hand under her elbow. "Now that we have that settled, can we move on and enjoy the party?"

She quirked an eyebrow. "What are you Silverwings offering?"

He guided her toward the food table, where he opened a bottle of blackberry juice while she helped herself to some cheese and vegetables. "How long have you been racing?" he asked easily.

She added a roll to her plate. "I started last spring. I'd never cycled competitively before I came to Arizona State. During my freshman year I took it up and became hooked."

"You're still a student, then?"

The question was a normal follow-up to what she'd said, but she couldn't hide her uneasiness. "No, I dropped out."

Actually she'd flunked out, but she never told anyone that, especially her father. He'd had a fit when he found out she'd taken time off from school to race bicycles. She could just picture his rage if he found out the absence from college was permanent.

Debra picked at the food on her plate. The cheese left a bitter taste in her mouth. Or was it the topic? "I needed to work at racing full-time. A full course load didn't leave me enough hours to practice."

Sterling accepted her information without the usual admonitions that she should have stayed in college. "You're fortunate to be able to do that."

"I also work for Ralph and Cindy in their cycle shop when we're not racing. If it weren't for them, I wouldn't be here today." She crunched on a baby carrot.

Sterling began to move them toward an empty sofa when someone tapped her on the shoulder. Debra turned to see one of her former teammates.

"Tough break today, Marilyn." The young woman's bike had broken down.

"I need to talk to you."

Debra couldn't mistake the urgency in the cyclist's voice. Marilyn stared at Sterling, obviously in awe of the pro.

"I used to ride with Marilyn's team," Debra explained after introducing her to Sterling.

"The biggest club in Arizona." Marilyn shook Sterling's hand and then turned to Debra. "Looks like you made the right move. You raced like a pro today."

"Thanks," Debra murmured, uncomfortable with the accolade.

"I came by to ask if you'd say something to our women about the race. They were kind of down after such a resounding defeat."

Debra set down her plate of food. "You shouldn't feel that way. After all, you were riding against a trade team. They have hours a day to get into shape."

"The others need to hear that. Come on over for a sec, will you?"

Debra glanced at Sterling with a look of apology, which he accepted with a nod. She smiled at Marilyn. "Lead the way."

Chapter Six

Sterling didn't want to let Debra go, but he empathized with the Phoenix women's desire to talk with the day's winner. That was exactly what *he* wanted too. He followed her to the corner of the room where the women were sitting on a couch and two chairs.

One of them slid over so Debra could join them. "We were proud of you today, especially acing out someone like Mary-Reva."

"How did you get over that hill? We saw you fall back and then zip ahead of the men," another woman asked Debra, but she eyed Sterling as she spoke.

Sterling settled on the arm of the couch next to Debra. The peach scent of her shampoo teased his senses.

"You've improved since riding with us," Marilyn commented. "What's your secret?"

Debra hesitated. "No offense, but riding with Tex and Red pushed me to better my times."

Several of the team members murmured among themselves, which Sterling could understand. Riding with men was a good approach; it had worked for Debra.

Debra elaborated. "In order to achieve, you need to aspire to something bigger or better than you already are."

He tried to listen to the strategies she shared with the other cyclists, but he found himself enjoying even more the warm cadence of her voice as she spoke. He admired her generosity. The guys were too cutthroat to share tactics.

Eddie and the others were across the room, laughing at some joke. He used to be right in there with them, feeding off the rush of victory. Not lately.

Sterling looked at Debra, and he saw the excitement in her eyes. Envy snaked into his soul. What was it she'd said? *You need to aspire to something bigger or better than you already are.* It had been at least a year since he had aspired to anything bigger, brand-new, or even exciting.

"We weren't enough competition for you?" Another woman spoke to Debra but smiled at Sterling. Sterling shifted position, braced one ankle over the other knee, and leaned closer to Debra. The woman turned away. *Good.* She'd caught on fast that he wasn't interested. He focused his attention on Debra.

"I rarely beat Tex or Red, so I always have to try harder."

"Doesn't that get discouraging?" another team member asked.

"Sure it does. But today's win made it all worthwhile."

The women could relate to that. Sterling heard a different tone in their murmurings this time.

Debra's tone had changed too, as she lowered her voice so that just those in their circle could hear. "You've got to talk your coach into letting you ride with the men. It won't slow them down."

"Works with us," Sterling inserted, glad to support Debra's claim. "Often we work out with the women from a local team. It gives us more incentive too."

"Why?" Marilyn asked. "Because you want to show off?"

Sterling chuckled. "That's part of it, but it has more to do with pride. No man wants to be beaten by a female cyclist."

Debra rolled her eyes. "How macho."

Marilyn nudged Debra. "Isn't that the trouble you had today with Davis?"

He could sense more than see Debra stiffen.

"Is he on your team?" she asked Marilyn.

"Joined this month. We heard what he did."

Sterling sat upright, placing both feet on the floor. "I hope he got reprimanded."

"Not by the team manager, but I heard some of the guys warning him off." Marilyn passed a tray of crackers to Sterling.

Sterling took the tray and passed it on to another woman who spoke out.

"Riders like that should be disqualified."

The woman across from him batted her eyes. "You were lucky that Sterling was around."

Debra agreed, but Sterling didn't. He didn't believe in luck. It *appeared* to have been luck that Eddie Smith's wheel had malfunctioned. It *appeared* to have been Debra's luck that Sterling happened to be in the right place at the right time. But Sterling knew it had nothing to do with luck. For that he was thankful.

Debra shrugged. "There's always going to be someone like Davis around. You learn to deal with it."

It was obvious that Debra had no interest in impressing him. Just sitting in this group, he could sense the difference in attitude between her and the other women.

Sterling wouldn't mind the female attention if he thought it was himself they were interested in, but experience had taught him that the name *Silverwing* attracted just as much if not more regard than the name *Sterling Wade.* Maybe that was why Debra interested him. She presented a challenge.

He took a bite of the cracker, barely noticing the salty tang of his favorite cheese. No, it was more than that. Debra's drive and enthusiasm drew him. Her sharing attitude fascinated him. Her wholesome beauty, a beauty that she didn't flaunt or use for her own ends, attracted him.

Most of the other women seemed more interested in flirting and games. Casual affairs didn't appeal to Sterling, which was why he usually kept himself aloof from the opposite sex during racing events. When he decided to go after a woman, it would be a serious matter, no game.

Debra smiled at something one of the women said. It might be time to become serious. He grinned as he listened to Debra talk. Yes, here was a woman who could possibly change the course of his interests. Too bad he had to leave in the morning. But for sure he would make it back to Tucson in time for the next meet.

The thought of leaving brought Sterling up short. He didn't have much time with Debra. He didn't want to waste any more on shoptalk.

"There are fewer people on the patio. Would you like to take a break and sit outside?"

The others stared. Debra didn't seem to notice—or care— that she had the exclusive attention of a Silverwing. Sterling grabbed her hand before she could refuse and helped her up. Yep, that's what he liked about her. No guile.

They wove past the refreshment table toward the French doors. Her hand felt right in his—soft yet strong. The rapid beat of salsa music drew them toward the patio. He pressed her fingers to the rhythm.

She pulled her hand away and paused. Sterling saw the hesitation in her features. "Something wrong?" he asked.

"I don't dance." She turned away from the doors.

He stepped in front of her to stave off her retreat. "You don't have to dance. You ride a bike well enough to make up for it. Let's just sit outside and watch."

Her obvious relief made him smile. He guided her over to the low brick wall enclosing the patio.

She hiked herself up onto the wall. Sterling sat next to her and reached for her hand. She started to pull back but changed her mind. Sterling kept his palm flat with her fingers resting on top. No threat.

She stared at their hands. "Why am I letting you do this?"

"I told you. I'm your Prince Charming."

Her mock groan included a reflex squeeze of her fingers. Her eyes locked with his, and Sterling forced himself not to react.

"I guess I did need rescuing back there. They were nice to talk to, but I don't really like crowds," she admitted.

"See? We have something else in common."

Her laughter blended with the fast-paced music. Her peach scent accented the fragrance of new spring flowers. Her eyes sparkled like the light of the stars in the dark sky overhead. Perfect. *Now, if only this moment could last . . .*

It didn't. She shifted and squirmed and finally withdrew her hand on the pretense of finding a more comfortable position on the wall. She braced her hands on either side of her and scooted back.

"Comfortable now?" he asked.

"Better." She smiled, and they both knew it was because her hand was free.

He shifted so that he was looking her almost directly in the eye. "I like you, Debra, but I won't force anything."

"That's why I'm sitting here. You understand how difficult it is to be involved on the road." Her eyes locked with his, and he could see sincerity and a hint of loneliness. "It's nice to be able to talk and not have to worry."

Don't let me ever do anything to lose that trust.

He smiled, resisting the urge to tuck a strand of her hair behind her ear. "I enjoy talking to you too. I'm hoping some of your enthusiasm will rub off on me."

Concern shadowed her features, and Sterling realized he'd said too much. He hoisted himself off the wall. "Wait here. I'll bring us some more juice."

Idiot. Admitting his faults wasn't the way to impress a woman. Quickly he pushed his way to the refreshment table, thankfully avoiding any detours.

Sorry he'd bailed out of the personal nature of the conversation, he hurried back to Debra with their drinks. He didn't want to take any chances that someone else would grab her attention. He breathed a sigh of relief when he saw her still sitting alone, watching the dancers swirling in front of her.

He paused, enjoying the sight of her beauty. Her jean-clad legs swung back and forth in time to the music. The dim lights around the patio were reflected in her shiny hair. A slight breeze lifted a few strands. He sighed. Too bad he had to leave for San Diego in the morning.

Making it back right away to the racing circuit seemed more of an unsure thing the more he listened to his father. Michael David Wade paced behind his mahogany desk. Sterling knew it was important to Coronado Industries that he was here, but he had a hard time working up much enthusiasm for the challenge.

"Are you sure Imperial Industries isn't behind this?" Sterling asked.

"I've had Joe on it since we got wind of the attempted buyout. He hasn't been able to trace it."

Sterling tapped the top of his briefcase. It felt strange to be in a suit and tie after a month in either Lycra skins or loose-fitting sweats. It was hard to keep his mind focused.

Debra. Her smile, her peach scent, her dark eyes. Forcing himself to concentrate, he checked the figures one more time.

The senior Wade pointed to the pile of papers. "We have no choice but to present this to the board."

Sterling took a sip of coffee, hoping the dark-roasted caffeine would help. "Maybe someone will slip up and leak a clue."

Michael smiled as he surveyed the large office, mentally preparing himself as he always did before a board meeting. It wouldn't be the first time Coronado Industries had come up against impossible odds and ended up triumphant.

"You've got to maintain that communication, son," Michael always advised him.

Sterling hoped communication between the two companies would be open now. Coronado could be in a serious bind. He wasn't really that worried, though. Cautious, perhaps. With the proper guidance, they had never been unable to handle a situation yet.

Michael's secretary entered the office and greeted his employers. "Everyone has arrived and been given refreshments and copies of the reports."

Michael thanked him and led the way into the boardroom, where shafts of sunlight filtered across the thick carpet. Sterling followed, inhaling the aroma of fresh-brewed coffee. He sat to his father's right and watched him smile from the head of the long table. He had to admire the man. With no sign of tension or stress, the senior Wade exuded confidence.

The meeting began, and an hour hadn't gone by before one of Sterling's cousins confessed his plan to sell out.

"At least give us the option for first bid," Sterling urged, clenching his fists under the table to hide his anger. Betrayal always hurt more when family was involved.

Hours passed before they closed the meeting. Sterling waited with his father as the board members filed out one by one.

When the door closed on the last one, Sterling stood and stretched. "It's over. Finally."

"There are still more details to iron out. Probably take a week or two."

Sterling inwardly groaned. The race in Tucson was this weekend. After that the Silverwings would head for California. He doubted Debra's team would be traveling that far. Teams their size usually stayed in the local region. He wouldn't be back in Arizona for two months.

"Don't look so grim, son. I can handle business from here on in."

"I can stay."

Michael laughed. "I'm reading you like a book. You're anxious to leave. What's up?"

Sterling shrugged, not yet wanting to discuss his interest in Debra.

"You didn't seem that hot to go out on the circuit this spring."

His thoughts so easily discerned, Sterling decided he might as well be honest. "I don't know what's gotten into me lately." He loosened his tie. "Maybe I'm burned out."

"That can happen. After all, practically your whole life revolves around the sport. Most of the year, anyway. Maybe you need other interests to round you out."

"I have my work here, I belong to a top team, I go to church. . . ."

"You already excel in all those areas. I'm talking about new passions, something that fills your heart, something that inspires and challenges you."

"Like your work with the kids in the *barrio?*"

Michael stood and paced in front of the windows, alerting Sterling that the elder Wade was deep in thought. "A man needs to give something back for all he has."

Sterling shifted uneasily. Of course his father was right. But projects like his father's efforts in the *barrio* took time—time Sterling needed to work out and keep in shape if he was going to continue to race.

His father stopped pacing and looked him in the eye. "What about a woman? You should be thinking about marriage, providing me and your mother with grandchildren."

Heat flushed his face, and Sterling knew the coloring would be noticed.

"Aha!" His father clapped his hands together. "You've met someone."

Sterling lifted his hands, but before he could speak a word of protest, Michael continued. "It's about time. Your mother and I were beginning to give up hope of having a grandchild."

"Don't go jumping the gun. I just met Debra."

"Must be some woman to get you so eager to leave home after only one day."

Sterling turned his back, went to the sideboard, and refilled his coffee cup.

"Who is she?"

"Her name's Debra Valenzuela. She races on a Phoenix team." He wasn't about to tell his father any more yet. He didn't really *know* much more yet, except for what his heart was telling him.

Michael's sigh filled the boardroom. "Guess that'll have to do for now. I can see you aren't ready to give out details."

"It's still brand-new. Might be best to just keep it between us men for now. Mom will—"

"She'd want to fly out and meet her."

"That's what I mean. Give me a chance before you and Mom scare her off."

Michael laughed good-naturedly. "I'll tell her—can't help that—but you're right: you need to handle this on your own." His face sobered. "But be careful. Don't rush into anything."

"Caution has been easy to practice—until I met Debra." Sterling finished his coffee and set the cup down. "Actually, I don't have many details to share yet, just an inner knowing that she's the one for me."

"Your insight is usually reliable, son. I say go for it."

Sterling closed his briefcase and snapped the locks. He planned to take his father's advice and do just that. "If I get going, I can catch this evening's flight to Tucson."

"Hold on. You aren't going to leave town without seeing your mother, are you?"

Sterling took a breath to calm himself. Debra had to work, so she wouldn't be around until Saturday. It was only Monday.

"You're right. Mom would have a fit, wouldn't she?"

"She'd be disappointed."

That did it. Sterling grinned. "You know how to rub in the salt. Sure. I'll stay over and see Mom. Maybe I'll head for the house now."

"We can drive out together." Michael stood. "And, son, there's something else you need to know."

Sterling eyed the frown on his father's face.

"Your mom invited a young lady to dinner."

Sterling groaned. "When is she going to stop trying to find me a wife?"

"When you find your own."

"Promise not to mention Debra to Mom this evening."

The mock grimace didn't worry Sterling. His father would keep silent. For tonight anyway.

Chapter Seven

Debra leaned against the Desert Cyclery van and squinted against the sun's glare. The weather had remained unexpectedly hot. Usually March was a perfect month to cycle in the Southwestern desert. Today's weather would work the cyclists into an energy-draining sweat.

"Make sure you put plenty of glucose into those water bottles," Debra reminded Cindy, who was inside the van sorting the equipment for her, Tex, and Red.

Ralph grabbed two bottles from Cindy and slipped them into the cages fastened to her bike frame. "Since they're racing the men separately from the women, Tex and Red won't be out there to help you."

"Speaking of men," Cindy said as she climbed out of the van, "we'd better get over to the sign-up table. They'll be starting the Senior Men's Category in twenty minutes."

"Tex and Red are all set," Ralph assured her. "I just left them talking to a group of Silverwings."

Sterling. Were they talking to him? As soon as the question formed, Debra dismissed it. The Silverwing had popped into her mind entirely too many times that week. His smile. His laughter. His "Prince Charming" ways. She hadn't wanted to be thinking of Sterling then, and she certainly didn't want to now. She needed her mind focused on the race.

In spite of her inner admonitions, Debra found herself peering toward the starting area in hopes of catching a glimpse of Sterling. Helmets glistened in the sun; team colors moved in waves as the men positioned themselves. Greens, pinks, reds, blues. She shifted onto tiptoe but couldn't see any sign of silver. Annoyed with herself for being disappointed, she turned away.

"Where's the stopwatch?" Cindy's question broke into Debra's thoughts.

Debra pointed toward the rear of the van where they'd set out their gear. "By the binoculars on the table."

"Right where you left them," Ralph teased as he lifted the shiny orb on a silver chain out of a pile of towels.

Debra barely registered the banter that quickly escalated between Ralph and Cindy. She was too busy trying to spot Sterling in the crowd of Seniors getting ready to race.

At the far end of the track, Debra saw the hot pink van of the Orange-Lite team. Across the side she could read their logo printed in fluorescent orange. In front of the van, Hugh Ashford stood talking to Mary-Reva.

Debra frowned slightly. The Orange-Lites had arrived early, but Ashford had made no attempt to speak to her. He'd watched her time trials last week but had made no comment one way or the other. Today, when she'd bicycled by the van, he hadn't even waved.

"He's concentrating on the race," Cindy had told her.

Debra decided to believe that, rather than fret about being slighted. If she wanted the manager's attention, she'd have to bring in another win. This afternoon during the women's race, she'd get her opportunity to do that.

"Going for another upset?"

The masculine voice came from directly behind her. Debra spun around to see Sterling coast up to the van, put his feet down, and straddle his Silverwing bicycle. A smile spread across her face.

"About as ready as I'm going to be. And you?" With appreciation, she eyed the picture he made on the sleek machine. "Looks like everything's in shape." She felt the flash of heat creep up her cheeks. "I didn't mean . . ."

Sterling grinned, not helping her out.

Debra adjusted her sunglasses, wishing they hid more of her face. Time to change the subject. "Ready to win?"

He continued to stare at her pink cheeks. "We'll miss you out there."

She didn't want to be missed. She didn't want to notice the Silverwing. Yet here she was, blushing to her roots, because all she could do was notice. She let the breeze whip her hair in front of her face, hoping it would hide the color.

Sterling gestured toward another cyclist waiting nearby. "Bet he won't miss you, though."

When the man lifted his head, Debra saw that it was Davis. She laughed, relieved that Sterling's attention was no longer on her.

"You planning to ride in the rear pack again?" she teased.

Sterling patted his bicycle. "Not unless there's some mechanical failure."

Debra eyed the bike with envy. "I can't imagine a bike like that having any problems."

"We try to work them out beforehand, but we can't control the roads." Sterling shifted his weight.

Debra quickly looked up, hoping he didn't notice that she was staring again. "The roads in Tucson are pretty decent."

"I've always liked Arizona. It's a bike-friendly state." He reached over and tucked a strand of her hair behind her ear. "Seems especially nice now."

Debra took a step back, uneasy with his touch. Not because she didn't like it, but because she did. Too much.

He dropped his arm and gripped his handlebars. "You been here all this week?" he asked. "I had to leave the team and fly to San Diego on business Monday."

"No. After the workout for Ashford, I worked in Tempe at Desert Cyclery," Debra explained, glad for another change of subject. "Customer service for Ralph and Cindy."

Sterling nodded and positioned his right foot on the pedal.

"Walk with me while I head for the sign-up table, and tell me about it."

She should stay here and let him focus on the race. She should stay here and get her mind on her own race. She should stay here and forget about Sterling Wade.

But she didn't. She grabbed her bike and walked beside him as he headed toward the starting area, where the other Seniors had gathered. "Actually I'm more like a gal Friday. You know, any odd jobs that come up."

She wanted to ask him what he did but decided not to. The less she knew about the Silverwing, the less involved she would be.

"Good place to work if you like cycling. I pretty much have a seasonal job myself to leave me free to race," Sterling said.

More interested than she wanted to be, she glanced over and smiled. "Some people think we're nuts." Her father did. "What does your family think about all this bicycling?"

"Let's say they have a vested interest in my racing."

What did that mean? Did they support him the way her brothers and sisters financed her? But no, he placed often. Of course, she had heard rumors that he wasn't placing lately.

Sterling paused, gripping his handlebars. "I see my team. Much as I hate to end this, I'd better head over there."

She should have wanted the encounter to end. But she didn't. "I need to find Ralph and Cindy." She could see Ralph giving Tex and Red some last-minute pointers. She stopped walking and straddled her bike. "Good luck today."

Sterling fastened his regulation helmet. " 'Luck' has nothing to do with it. But I'll take any prayers."

"You don't think you have the skill to win?"

He winked and sent her a smile that made her forget her question. "I always do my best. Can't ask more of a person than that."

His best should place him within the top ten cyclists. Would hers give her the win?

Shouts began to rumble across the group of Seniors. There had to be over a hundred gathered at the starting line. Debra had stalled long enough. She glanced one more time in Sterling's direction and hopped onto her bike seat.

"Ride tough." She tapped his handlebars and then began to weave her way to the sidelines of the crowd.

The next fifteen minutes were waves of motion in a sea of color as the men in the Senior Category positioned themselves for the race to begin. Cleated shoes clicking onto pedals, the flash of helmets and sunglasses in the sun, the reflection of neon colors boasting logos on Lycra shorts and shirts—these were sights and sounds Debra loved. Sights and sounds that made her pulse race with the anticipation of competition.

Experienced cyclists rode with the pros. Ages ranged from eighteen to thirty. There were some veterans who hung in past their thirties but very few. It wasn't so much their age that took them out of the races but their lack of time to work out. By the time they reached their late twenties, they usually had families to support, jobs that took their time, and children to raise.

Debra glanced at Sterling. Did he want those things?

Cindy came up beside her and pointed out Tex and Red. They had good positions. The starting gun exploded into the desert air. Startled birds flew upward in fright. In the background saguaro cacti stood like sentinels guarding the desert as the wave of color moved into action.

Debra watched Sterling until he was out of sight. With determination she forced him out of her mind. If she was going to win, she had to focus on her race now. She studied the road. She wanted to see how the remaining bicycles took the bumps and curves. A pothole could cost critical seconds.

"Too bad you won't be able to see the end of this race," Cindy commented. "They moved up your time. You'll be starting just before they make it back in."

"Think we'll get into any lagging packs?" Debra liked to practice with the men, but she didn't like to race with them.

Most of the riders who lagged behind were amateurs. Some of them didn't know or chose not to follow the subtle rules or code of ethics. Like Davis.

Cindy shook her head. "You'll be fine. The first stretch is hills and curves. By the time you women clear the pass, the stragglers will be home."

Mary-Reva and the Orange-Lite team cruised by. "They've been out practicing all week," Debra groaned. "Lucky them, they don't have to work."

Cindy tugged on Debra's race number to straighten it. "Don't get negative on me. You've ridden this course more times than they have. You've got the advantage of being used to the heat too."

The reminder improved Debra's spirits, until she saw Hugh Ashford walk by. Even though he'd only been twenty feet away, he didn't wave. He must not have been impressed with her workout last Monday.

His slight served to make her more determined. She began tucking her hair under her helmet. "I'm going to win."

Cindy clapped her on the back. "Atta girl."

Ralph yelled for Cindy to join him.

"We're going to be at the pass for Tex and Red. We'll wait there for you too."

Debra nodded. "That's going to be the critical part of the race. I'm glad you'll be there."

"Once you come over the pass, it's a straight shot into the finish," Cindy reminded her. "So be sure you're in a good position by then. Mary-Reva's team can maneuver you away from the lead if they're with you."

Debra took a deep breath and pictured the road. She imagined where she'd be on every inch. Pulling ahead at the right time would bring her victory.

It seemed like hours before the women's class began. Debra hoped that, with the men out on the road, she would be able to stop thinking of Sterling. His smile. His touch. They kept sneaking into her mind. She forced herself to push away thoughts of the Silverwing, but then those deep, unexplainable longings would haunt her instead. She maneuvered to the start, hoping the activity there would clear her head.

Several women she didn't recognize were in the lineup. Unlike the men's groups, the women weren't categorized by age. There never were enough women competitors to do so, but trade teams like the Orange-Lites were helping build the Stateside image of the sport.

The gun exploded with a loud pop, and Debra began in a good starting position. It didn't take long, however, before the Orange-Lites began to maneuver. They didn't want Debra to find a break in their ranks to exploit. She was the only real threat to Mary-Reva. Just as they were about to "close the gate" on her, Marilyn sprinted into a gap and left it open. It appeared that Debra was going to get some help after all.

"We'll ride with you as long as we can hold up." Marilyn nodded toward two other riders from her team. "After that you're on your own."

"Thanks," Debra yelled. "Keep me covered."

The echelon wound its way up the hill. Marilyn and her team poured out everything they had. Debra knew that they would never be able to keep up the pace. They were sacrificing the race to give her a chance.

"We Arizonans have to stick together," Marilyn puffed.

Mary-Reva came up beside Debra. "You're covered now, but we'll get you at the top."

The comment was just the spur Debra needed to drive her onward. In spite of the climb coming up, it would be to her advantage to go for a sprint now.

After checking to make sure Mary-Reva's attention was elsewhere, Debra reached over and tapped Marilyn on the knee. Her friend nodded. No words had to be spoken. She knew what to do.

Marilyn signaled the other members of her team. Carefully, they maneuvered into position at the front of the echelon.

When Debra was ready to go, they would be in position to block the Orange-Lites from following.

Debra smiled as she watched Marilyn's team file into position. The Orange-Lites would not be expecting her to get help from another team. They were so busy watching Debra, they missed seeing the setup.

One more position and Debra would be ready to go. Quickly she took a sip of glucose. Energy surged into her system. She powered down and was on her way.

The groans and shouts from the women made the effort worthwhile. Now they would see what an asset she'd be to their team. She was a rider who took advantage of every situation.

The move was to her benefit, but it didn't come without a high cost. Her lungs ached with each breath. Her leg muscles burned from the gradual climb. If she could keep the lead until the downhill, she'd have it made. No one would be able to catch her on the straightaway.

Throwing her bike side to side, Debra pressed on. Shouts behind her let her know that Marilyn and the others had dropped out of the pack. Now Mary-Reva would be a threat. Her team would provide a draft for Mary-Reva to conserve her energy.

"Don't give out on me now, body," she murmured as she glanced over her shoulder.

Mary-Reva was closing in.

When Debra hit the downhill stretch, the wind whistled in her ears, drowning out the shouts of the fans.

Cacti and brush blurred as Debra streamlined her body into the wind. She had a straight shot now. But if Mary-Reva caught up to her wheel, Debra would have to force a final sprint to the finish.

Sterling locked his bicycle, grabbed an atom bottle—a concoction of Coke and water mixed for a quick energy shot of sugar and caffeine—and hurried back to the finish line. He didn't want to miss out on the women's class finish. Debra had been on her own this time. Would she win?

"Way to go." Tex and Red slapped him on the back and congratulated him as he joined the two Desert Roadrunners.

Sterling nodded, barely paying attention to the fact he'd only placed ninth. *Debra.* Where was she?

"Have you heard any word?" he asked Tex.

"Rumor's out that Debra made the pass in the lead."

Impressed, Sterling felt his pulse speed up a notch. "Anyone close to her?"

"Heard Mary-Reva and her team were closing in."

Sterling fought the urge to jump onto his bicycle and go see for himself. His presence would only create a distraction.

"Go, go," he murmured instead, twisting his fingers around the plastic bottle.

Tex shifted impatiently from one foot to the other. "I can't believe she's acing out the Orange-Lites twice now."

The crowd became restless.

"They're on their way in." Sterling strained his neck to see. "Let's head over there where we can spot her."

The three men edged toward the finish line in time to see a flash of kelly green followed by hot pink.

Tex shouted as he jumped up. "She won!"

Red started running toward Debra. "Can you believe she came in first?"

Sterling followed closely behind, ready to give her the atom bottle filled with quick energy.

Debra circled the parking lot and headed toward the men.

Before her teammates could get to her, Sterling moved ahead and held her bike by the handlebars after she came to a stop. "That was some finish."

Her smile was filled with triumph. In spite of the perspiration dripping down her neck and the look of strain in her features, she looked gorgeous.

"Here." He handed her the atom bottle. "You could use this. Caffeine, glucose, and water."

She grimaced at the taste but drank the energy booster down. "I don't normally go for these."

Sterling had to step aside while her two teammates gave her a hug. Ralph and Cindy arrived. Fans and spectators crowded around the winner. He could see he needed to step back.

Hugh Ashford strolled over and congratulated her. "Aced us out again." He shook his head in mock dismay.

Debra shrugged as if the win meant nothing to her, but Sterling noticed she was paying close attention to the Orange-Lite manager.

"I want to talk to you," Ashford told her. "How about dinner tonight?"

Sterling's heart dropped when she accepted his offer. He bit the inside of his cheek to keep quiet and not interfere.

Once he had what he wanted, Ashford returned to Mary-Reva and the rest of the Orange-Lites, who were nursing their pride. Being beaten by an amateur made them nervous.

A protective urge coursed through Sterling as he remained close to Debra. Too bad he couldn't find a way to get her to cancel her date with Ashford.

Chapter Eight

Debra floated through the rest of the day in a haze. She barely remembered cleaning her bike. Cindy's excited chatter blurred with her rubdown. Not only had she beaten Mary-Reva Brown and her team, she'd been invited out by their manager. This could only mean one thing.

She'd soon be on her road to success.

At the motel where she shared the room with the other Desert Roadrunners, Debra hurried through her shower. She tried to focus on her upcoming dinner with Hugh Ashford, but thoughts of Sterling crept, unwanted, into her mind.

Steam filled the small bathroom, making it difficult to get ready. The dampness threatened to wilt her bright yellow dress. Debra opened the door to clear the air. Cindy and the others waited in the crowded room for their turn in the shower. They planned to attend the party put on by one of the local teams but had no time crunch like Debra.

"Think Ashford'll bring you to the party when you're done with dinner?" Tex asked as he propped his feet on one of the beds.

Red knocked Tex's feet off and put his own up. "Everyone's going to wonder where today's star is."

"Just tell them she's out. No need to mention with whom." Cindy patted the bed next to her for Debra to join her. "Don't go giving Debra a bad time. This is her big opportunity."

"You be careful," Tex advised. "I've heard rumors about the guy. He takes advantage of young women who want to try out for his team."

Sterling had said the same thing. A brief wave of anxiety washed through Debra. She shook it off. Both men were overly protective.

She ran her brush through her hair and sat beside Cindy, who had offered to put it in a French braid. "I can take care of myself."

Cindy took over the brushing. "Ashford has a reputation with women he dates, but he has a strict code with his own team."

"You can say that again." Red whistled. "I tried to talk to Mary-Reva. I couldn't get within ten feet of her."

Ralph turned down the volume of the television so he could join in. "He won't allow his women to date while touring the circuit. He says men interfere with their concentration."

"What if one of them gets serious during the winter— becomes engaged or something?" Debra asked.

"He doesn't care what they do off-season." Ralph sat back down and continued. "But they have a clear understanding that there will be no contact once the races begin."

So why do I keep thinking about that Silverwing?

Debra winced when Cindy pulled a hair. She had no business talking to Sterling or even thinking about him, not if she wanted to join the Orange-Lite team.

"I remember last year there was a rider who was engaged. Remember, Ralph?" Cindy set down the brush. "She wanted to see her fiancé so bad. I guess she got into an awful row with Ashford. He let her go."

"In the middle of the season?" Debra asked, wondering if there might be a possibility for an opening this summer.

"He won't bend his rules."

"Debra, you sure you want to be constrained by a team manager like that?" Red asked, as he tossed a pillow at Tex.

Debra held out a yellow ribbon for Cindy to weave into the braid. "It so happens I agree with him. You need your full concentration out there. If you join a national team, you should commit to your cycling."

"Whoa!"

"Tough lady."

Tex and Red hooted and hollered, but Debra ignored their teasing. She knew what she wanted. She knew she was right, which was why her recurring thoughts of Sterling disconcerted her so.

"Besides," Debra continued, "I don't have much choice. I can't afford to get to all the major races. The Orange-Lites coming to Arizona for these two events gave me a chance to become known by a professional team."

Tex and Red quieted down. They could relate to that. The cyclists were just as excited to race with the Silverwings. They had their dreams too.

"This is a big opportunity for you." Ralph rolled up the *TV Guide* and tapped his knee with the end of it to emphasize his point. "Which is why Cindy and I have decided to try to pick up a couple more team members and enter you in the district level races in Southern California."

Debra stood, ruining Cindy's efforts with the braid. "Are you serious? We'll be racing with pro teams all month?"

"And next month too," Cindy pointed out, as she pushed Debra back down and started again with her hair. "You'll be in great shape for the National Prestige Classic in Bisbee."

Debra couldn't sit still. She pulled away from Cindy again and hopped around the room with Tex and Red. *La Vuelta de Bisbee* had been a sure thing because it was in Arizona. But it wasn't until the end of April, almost two months away. She had been worried about letting so much time pass before seeing Ashford again. Now she would be racing right along with the Orange-Lites.

And the Silverwings.

Debra dismissed the thought of Sterling. Again.

Cindy chuckled as she patted the end of the bed where Debra had been sitting. "Get over here so I can finish your braid. We're going to a lot of trouble for you. You can't blow it with Ashford now by showing up with your hair half done."

Cindy was teasing, but her remarks sobered Debra. "I appreciate this. It's going to be tough getting us to California."

"We think you have a good chance of making a national team."

"Good advertising for us." Ralph stood up and paced while puffing out his chest and pretending his offer was no big thing.

Debra reached out and grabbed Ralph's hand as he passed by. "I can pay for a couple of the trips. After all, I won cash prizes last week and today."

"You need to use that money on yourself." Cindy emphasized her point with a tug on the braid. "With prospects of winning, we can pick up some new sponsors."

Debra let go of Ralph's hand and held her head still. "At least let me chip in on the gas."

"We'll see," was all she and Ralph would concede.

Tex and Red began sparring with fake punches. "We can help too."

Ralph raised a hand to quiet them down. "Let's just get through one weekend at a time."

Cindy tied the ends of the ribbon in a big yellow bow that brushed against Debra's bare neck. "Right. Like getting you ready for your date."

"This is not a 'date,' " Debra reminded Cindy. "It's business. Remember?"

Tex walked over and tapped her on the shoulder. "Sure hope Wade knows that. He didn't seem too pleased that you were going out with Ashford."

"Sterling's a friend. Period."

"He'd like to be more," Red teased as he tossed a pillow at Tex, barely missing Debra. He laughed. "And so would you. Admit it."

The news report that came onto the television screen saved Debra from a response. Ralph turned up the volume. Conversation died as the cyclists listened to the weather report. Debra retreated into her thoughts.

Sure, she wanted more than friendship with Sterling, but not now, when she was so close to her dream. She had to make the Orange-Lite team. It was the only thing she could think of that would appease her father. Their phone conversation earlier in the day proved that he needed something to make him proud of her.

"Papá. *I won today. A district race.*"

"*District race. National race. Does it give you the money to pay the rent? Does it—*"

"*I won five hundred dollars.*"

"*And what will five hundred dollars buy you these days?*"

"*New tires, a—*"

"*Don't get smart,* mi hija. *You go back to school, or at least come home. Your* mamá *misses you. Maybe she can talk some sense into your stubborn head.*"

"*Let me talk to* Mamá *now.*"

At least her mother had been excited about her win. It was small consolation. If Debra could race with a professional team, she'd show her father what a big deal competitive bicycling was.

Cindy's voice broke into her thoughts. "Your hair looks great. All you need now is a smile."

Debra gave her one.

"That's better."

She hugged the older woman. "Thanks, Cindy."

"Be careful tonight," Cindy whispered.

By the time Debra put on her light lipstick, Hugh Ashford was knocking at their door. While Ralph and the others greeted him, she checked her appearance one last time as best she could in the small bathroom mirror.

The bright yellow dress accented the golden color of her skin. The style was simple yet flattering. She hoped it was dressy enough for where Hugh planned to take her. Shrugging, she left the room. It would have to do. It was all she had with her.

At first, during the drive through town, Debra was nervous, but Hugh's easygoing attitude soon made her feel comfortable. Once inside the Old Tucson restaurant, she knew the dress she had worn was perfect.

He seated her near the fountain. "It's always a pleasure to take out a beautiful woman."

"This is business, right?"

"Of course." He sat across from her. "But I do sometimes like to mix pleasure with business."

"That's not what I hear. I thought you kept strict regulations with your team."

"Ah, but you're not on the team." He smiled and reached for her hand. "Yet."

Debra grabbed her napkin and placed it and her hands in her lap. "That's why I'm here, though, right? To discuss the prospects."

Hugh shrugged as he picked up the wine list. "If you say so. Shall we celebrate your victory with champagne?"

Debra couldn't believe her ears. The Orange-Lites had a strict code against alcohol, as did the Silverwings.

"Are you trying to knock me out of the competition for the time trials tomorrow?"

His laugh sounded hollow and insincere. "Would that be sporting of me?"

"I don't drink."

The frown that crossed Hugh's features was brief. Debra glanced around the restaurant, suddenly glad to be in a crowded room.

"What would you like?"

"Some of this citrus blend sounds good. It should go well with Mexican food."

They ordered chimichangas, flautas, and peppered steak. Debra had no trouble enjoying the spicy food; the company was another matter.

Debra tried again to return the conversation to bicycling. "Where are the Orange-Lites racing next?"

"We're headed for California. But I'm more interested in where we're going after dinner."

"There's the party put on by the Tucson club."

"Or there's my room at the hotel."

Debra almost choked on her tortilla. "Excuse me?"

Hugh's brow furrowed. "I didn't invite you out just to talk shop."

Debra placed what was left of her tortilla onto her plate. "I'm sorry you had the wrong impression. I'm here for one reason only. I want to be considered for the Orange-Lite team. I'm good. These last two races proved it."

Hugh laid his fork and knife down with studied care. "Let's get something straight. My teams are selected during fall tryouts. The team is set for this year. You can't bribe your way on to the team with a pretty smile."

Debra gasped. "You invited me out to discuss racing. Or so I thought. I have no desire to 'bribe' you. When I make a pro team"—she placed her fists on the table for emphasis—"and believe me, Hugh Ashford, I will, it will be on my merit as a cyclist. Not because I go to any team manager's hotel room." She pointed a finger at him. "And furthermore, I know for a fact that you don't allow relationships on tour, and you especially don't involve yourself with your cyclists."

In spite of their argument, she saw respect flash in his eyes. *Good.* They understood each other.

"You've made your point," he conceded. "You're an impressive cyclist. But it's early in the season. We'll see how you hold up, and then, come this fall . . ." He shrugged. "Who knows?"

It was all she could hope for. Yet a weight of uneasiness settled in her stomach. Would her chances be better if she'd said yes to his offer to go to his room? Had Mary-Reva and the others been chosen for the team that way?

The idea discouraged her. As much as she wanted to ride with the Orange-Lites, she knew she would never go that far. Sterling had been right about Ashford. Maybe she'd have better opportunities with the other teams.

However, the Orange-Lites were one of the few teams that

went to Europe and the only pro team from the Southwest. Getting exposure to the other teams was next to impossible at this point in time. She needed to stick with the Orange-Lites. She'd have to hope that what she'd heard about Ashford's integrity as far as his team members were concerned was true.

"I'd like to go to the party after dinner." She ate another bite of steak, determined to at least be well fed for the ordeal. "Ralph and Cindy can take me back to the motel afterward."

It would free him in case he wanted to pick someone else up at the party. Strangely enough, the thought of seeing Sterling appealed to her. Yet she didn't really want to have to explain to him what had happened. The experience was humiliating enough without having to share it.

Sterling mingled with the crowd, restless and tense. Several times he tried to join in the camaraderie and rehash the day's race. Boredom set in before he could put in his two cents' worth. He wouldn't have come, except maybe Ashford would drop by with Debra.

Thoughts of Hugh Ashford rumbled through his brain like a tired movie. What was the team manager up to? Why had Debra gone out with him? Why had Ralph and Cindy Robbins let her go?

The questions plagued him as he struggled to appear to be enjoying himself.

Eddie Smith came over and handed him a cran-raspberry drink. "You seem down, good buddy. You sulking because I aced you out of first?"

Sterling laughed for the first time that evening. "You caught a break for once, and you know it," he joked.

" 'Catching a break' plays no part in my superior skill."

" 'Superior skill'? Now, if you want *that,* you need to look *my* way." The joking words rang hollow. The way he'd been riding lately wouldn't inspire a flea.

But Eddie laughed, and the banter lifted Sterling's spirits somewhat. Eddie moved on to talk to Mary-Reva. Sterling paced in front of the refreshment table, barely aware of the smells of spicy meatballs and the clink of glasses.

For the umpteenth time he shot a look at the front door. It wasn't like Ashford to leave his cyclists unchaperoned. What was he doing?

Unable to stand another minute of waiting around, Sterling decided to leave. There were no guarantees that Ashford would even show up. And he didn't need to feed his overactive imagination with images of Ashford and Debra together.

Sterling didn't bother to say any good-byes. Better to leave and not have to answer questions. He tossed his empty juice bottle into a bin in the kitchenette and headed out the door. He punched the elevator button and then punched it two more times, pacing in between.

The light above the door turned green, and a muted *ding* sounded. Impatient to be on his way, Sterling moved directly in front of the door.

The door slid open, and, expecting the car to be empty, Sterling stepped inside. And froze.

Pressed into a corner of the elevator, Hugh Ashford was bent intently over Debra. Had they been kissing?

Pain shot through his heart as he gasped for breath.

Ashford looked up at the sound. "Looks like we have company. What's up, Wade? Leaving the party so soon?"

Chapter Nine

*S*terling. *Oh, no.* She didn't want him to see her with Ashford, but she didn't want him to leave either.

"You all right, Debra?" Even though he was beside her in the still-open elevator, Sterling's voice sounded as if it were coming from deep within a tunnel.

She felt shaken, her nerves ragged.

Ashford straightened and forced a smile—a smile that didn't reach his eyes. "We only had dinner. No need to get all bent out of shape."

Sterling stepped protectively toward Ashford and her but kept a fingertip on the door-open button. "Are you getting out, Ashford?" he asked pointedly.

Ashford glared at Sterling, then at Debra. She held her breath, still gripping the handrail that stretched around the elevator.

Ashford shifted his weight, and Sterling stepped back to let him out.

A harsh laugh escaped the team manager's lips before he pushed his way past Sterling and out of the car.

Debra's knees weakened. Sterling released the button and grasped her shoulders as the elevator door closed with a *whoosh*.

He looked into her eyes. "You're as pale as a ghost. If he hurt you—"

Debra stared at Sterling's chest, longing to curl into the safety of his arms. She gripped the rail until her knuckles turned white.

"He tried to kiss me is all." She breathed in. "Nothing happened. Sure glad you arrived, though."

He brushed back a strand of her hair that had escaped the braid and cupped her cheek in his hand. "That's my job. Prince Charming and all that."

She turned her face away. "I'm just a little shaken. That's all." Her lips trembled, and shivers raced through her. "You were right, though. About him."

"Do you want to go back to your motel?"

She pulled away from him and straightened the folds of her dress with her damp palms. "No, I'd still like to go to the party."

She took a deep breath and managed a tremulous smile. "Were you leaving already?"

"No. I was looking for you."

"Good. Will you escort me in? I could use a gallant knight about now."

Sterling relaxed and smiled. His silver-gray eyes softened, and he tucked her arm into his as he once more pressed the door-open button on the panel. "Come, my lady. The ball awaits your royal presence."

A weight seemed to be lifted off her shoulders. " 'Royal presence'? Aren't you exaggerating a bit?"

"Hey. You're the first-place winner today. That entitles you to special privileges." He guided her down the hall.

Special privileges. Hugh Ashford had thought they were his. A shiver of unease coursed through her. Did Sterling think the same thing?

Before she could contemplate further, he led her from the silence in the hall into a noisy suite filled with loud voices and laughter. People crowded together and filled every inch of space. Debra hesitated until Sterling let go of her arm and placed his hand at her back. The casual act and the warmth and strength of his fingers eased the sudden bout of anxiety.

He headed toward his team, gathered in one of the corners of the large suite. "The Silverwings are over there."

Debra spotted Tex and Red and relaxed, knowing they would be watching out for her also. "This is some spread." She gestured at the table filled with platters of food.

Sterling led her toward the table. "This racing club puts on one of the best parties. That's why the Silverwings like to come to Tucson to compete."

She trailed her fingers along the lace tablecloth, glad the conversation had turned to racing. "I thought it was the big purse that drew the professional teams."

"That too." Sterling winked and picked up a couple of bottles of Perrier.

Debra glanced toward Hugh and saw him talking to one of the women from the Tucson club. From the body language and the way the woman smiled, it was more than just a hospitable chat. It hadn't taken long for him to find another interest.

Debra turned back toward Sterling. He cared, but he wasn't hustling her. Not like Ashford had. She usually shied away from one-on-one contact at these parties, but somehow she felt safe and protected with Sterling. Not wanting to analyze why, she reached for the drink he offered.

"Regrets?"

"Relief." She took the cool bottle and touched it to her cheek. She was among friends now, and nothing had actually happened between her and Hugh. "Although I've probably lost my chance to place on the Orange-Lite team."

He stepped in front of her, blocking her view of the team manager. Sterling appeared calm, but Debra could see his fingers tighten around his bottle of Perrier. "You sure nothing happened back there?"

"I disappointed him, that was all. He was interested in sex. I was interested in bicycling."

"That must have come as a surprise to his ego." Sterling slid her elbow under his and moved with her through the crowd.

Debra knew she should want to pull free, but his nearness and take-charge confidence comforted her frazzled nerves. "I had no intentions of deflating anyone's ego."

Sterling sidestepped a couple sitting on the floor. "Does that mean mine is safe too?"

Debra grabbed his arm to keep her balance. "As long as you don't expect more than friendly conversation."

Once around the couple, he glanced back at her. "Ouch! You injured it already."

Debra laughed at his mock wounded look. She could easily become addicted to Sterling's brand of charm. Too easily.

Time to change the subject back to cycling. "All is not lost as far as finding a pro team. Ralph and Cindy promised they would take the Desert Roadrunners to the races in California."

Sterling paused and looked at her. "The larger clubs in the Pacific states offer bigger prize money and consequently draw major teams."

"What other women's teams will be racing?"

Sterling continued across the obstacle course to the other side of the room. "Think your chances might be better with them?"

"It doesn't hurt to make contacts. The only problem is that none of those teams race in Europe."

"Stick to the official tryouts. Ashford isn't bad as a manager. As much as I hate to give him credit for anything, he does have a code of ethics when it comes to the team."

"I really want to race in Europe."

"Then don't give up on the Orange-Lites because of tonight. He may have been testing you. Continue to ride as well as you have been. Ashford wants winners."

The comment gave her hope, even though she still felt disgust at the memory of the conversation at dinner. "Do you honestly think I could work with him?"

"Once you're on the team, you won't have to worry about him or any other man getting in your way."

Debra glanced at Sterling and wondered how he felt about that. How did she feel, for that matter? She could easily imagine spending time with Sterling. Could she manage knowing him now and then having to go a year without seeing him? Best to keep their involvement on a friendship level.

Sterling continued talking as he helped her maneuver around another couple. "You're right, though. There might be other pro teams from back east. They sometimes make the international races, so it wouldn't hurt to look them over when you're in California."

"Do you know any of the managers?"

Sterling turned to face her, his expression serious. "Sure. I can introduce you."

Debra hurried to explain, hoping he wouldn't notice the flush of heat rising up her neck to her cheeks. "I'm not asking you to do me any favors. I just wondered if you could tell me a little about them."

"Don't get all uptight on me now. In this business, contacts help."

"Thank you, but I wouldn't want to infringe on our friendship." Trying to hide her embarrassment, she sipped her chilled drink.

Sterling placed his hand under her elbow and guided her to a secluded spot near a large picture window. "At least we've progressed from shoptalk to friendship," he teased.

She studied his chiseled features, the warm smile, the eyes that revealed so much caring. "I have no time for involvements," she said sadly. "I'd think you would agree. You're known for staying unattached on the circuit too."

"That was true in the past. People change."

Debra shivered in spite of the warmth in the room. "If you're trying to flatter me now, implying that you're changing because of me, it won't work."

"Actually, it has a lot to do with cycling in general. My priorities seem to be shifting. After all, I've been racing for over ten years."

"Are you saying you're burned out? That's hard to imagine." But Debra guessed she had targeted the problem when she saw him wince. "Maybe you should take off for a season? Try another sport or another pursuit?"

A deep sense of loss coursed through her at the thought of not seeing Sterling again. She wanted to reach for his hand, but she grasped the folds of her skirt instead. She looked into his silver-gray eyes. They reflected the seriousness of his thoughts.

He shifted until he leaned against a wall. "I've given that some consideration. Trouble is, when you've been riding as long as I have, you wonder what else there is to do. I can't picture myself doing anything else."

She longed to have an answer for him. "Maybe another aspect of cycling, then. Working with a team. Promoting races."

His expression lightened. "No way. I'm not sure I'm gifted with enough patience for those tasks."

Debra understood not being gifted in many areas. "I would have guessed that you were."

"If that's a compliment, I'll take it."

"You've been very patient with Tex and Red. They appreciate all the pointers you gave them today. In fact, we couldn't get them to shut up about it."

He pulled away from the wall and shrugged. "That was no big thing. They're fun to work with. Their enthusiasm makes up for what they don't know yet."

"Give them another couple of years, and they'll be out there with the pros."

He smiled. "That wouldn't surprise me. Seems to be a trait that runs in your team."

Debra smiled back. "I want to win. Sure, it's a real high." But she had other reasons that were more important.

"I wouldn't be surprised to see you at the top. In fact, if you continue to ride like you have these past two weekends, all of the women's teams will be paying close attention to you."

Before she could respond, Eddie Smith strode over. "Hey, Wade, what strategy do you think . . ."

Debra barely paid attention to Eddie's question. Her thoughts were focused on Sterling's last comment.

Could that be true? Would the women's pro teams want her?

It appeared Sterling had predicted accurately. For the next two months, Debra placed in each race the Desert Roadrunners attended in California. Not first every time. She didn't have much chance when the teams worked together to get one of their members into the lead. However, in spite of their concerted efforts, she did place in the money and won several individual events. To her delight, team managers were paying close attention.

"Ashford came to talk to Ralph again today." Cindy broke the news as she pushed on Debra's stiff muscles.

Debra grimaced, more from the news than the pain in her legs. She shifted her position on the massage table. "He never says a word to me."

Cindy poured more oil into her hands and rubbed them together. The almond scent calmed Debra's nerves as the moisture soothed her skin. "And why would he? You made it clear you were only interested in business. Which was a smart move, by the way."

"Are you going to keep me in suspense? What did he say?"

"He's impressed with your wins. He asked Ralph if he thought you could make the grade as a pro."

Anticipation undid the relaxing ministrations of Cindy's massage. Debra sat upright. "I can't believe he's still interested."

Cindy laughed and pushed Debra onto her back. She started rubbing down her left leg. "Oh, he's interested, all right. He's considering you for his team. That's why he steers clear of you."

She paused, and Debra lifted her head to see a pensive look on her friend's face. "What else?"

Cindy hesitated and then shrugged. "He wanted to know if you were still free of . . . a relationship."

Debra started to rise, but Cindy pushed her back down and continued rubbing her legs.

"Don't worry. He's not interested in you personally. He just wants to be sure you're free to travel with the team."

Debra barely felt the tug and pull of Cindy's fingers. Thoughts clashed in her mind. Longings surged. She wanted to race pro. Had to. To prove herself to *Papá*. But what about Sterling? What about the new longings that surfaced every time the Silverwing was near? Debra took a deep breath, forcing the yearnings aside.

"Managers from two other teams talked to me today after my win. If Ashford doesn't pick me next season, I could have a chance with them." *And I still wouldn't be able to date Sterling.*

Cindy started rubbing down Debra's right leg. Debra forced herself to focus on the pain of her muscles instead of the pain that plagued her heart. Cindy's talk of racing helped.

"It makes a difference now that you have some team support. The managers can see that you know how to work with other cyclists. That's important."

Marilyn and some of the women who had helped her in Tucson were now riding with the Desert Roadrunners. Their presence made a big difference. Ralph's intensive training was quickly bringing them to a point where they could provide Debra with group backing.

Debra rolled over onto her stomach. "Once I started winning, the pros began cutting me off. It helps to have the team support. I couldn't win without them."

"So tell me, are these wins helping with that inner hunger we talked about?"

Debra tucked her head into the crook of her arms and groaned. "I thought for sure the longings would at least start to go away with each win bringing me closer to success. Maybe I need to actually be on a pro team before I feel a difference."

Cindy rubbed hard just below Debra's knee. "That's not going to do the trick. You've got your body and mind in shape. It's your spirit that is undernourished."

Debra lifted her head and placed fists under her chin. "You sound like Sterling."

"He's a caring and spiritual man. I couldn't pick anyone better for you myself. A relationship with him would help you out on many levels."

Debra's heart pounded, and her breath caught. Heat rushed from her neck into her cheeks. Sterling could ease some of the yearnings, but what about *Papá?* What about accomplishing her goals? "No. You're wrong. A relationship with Sterling will never happen. Not now anyway. I've got to go pro."

"We'll see. For now, just keep on placing like you're doing, and you'll be fine." Cindy swatted Debra's rear, the signal that she was finished with the massage and the conversation.

Debra had every intention of winning races. Pressure from home built with each month she stayed out of school, and she needed to pull off the big wins to appease her family. Her brothers and sisters would indulge her for only so long. So far they continued to support her efforts. At least with her wins, she didn't need their financial help. For now anyway. And if she went pro, she could eventually pay them back.

The next big race was the National Prestige Classic in Bisbee, Arizona. Debra would have an advantage because she could work out on the course before the race. In fact, the Desert Roadrunners had bypassed another California race in order to spend the weekend before *La Vuelta de Bisbee* practicing in the small town in southeast Arizona.

Marilyn puffed as she pulled beside Debra on the grade. "I'm sure glad Ralph insisted we come out here."

"These roads are terrible," Debra agreed.

The hilly road, one of the toughest on the Western circuit, wound its way up several long grades along Brewery Gulch through the main part of the rustic mining town situated in the hills. The route wound past each of the levels of the school built on infamous High School Hill. Narrow roads out of town created dangerous conditions.

In spite of or maybe because of the danger, Bisbee continued to sponsor the race.

"Hang in there!" Cindy yelled at the cyclists from the back of the van as Ralph drove ahead of them.

Debra made a face. "Easy for you to say. Why don't you cycle with us and see how it feels?"

"Then who would give you your massage?" Cindy quipped, not letting the remark faze her.

"Maybe we'll get a Silverwing to give them to us." Marilyn laughed. "I bet Sterling would give Debra one."

Debra groaned at the teasing. "Oh, please! He's just a friend."

Marilyn pulled her bike from side to side. "He's interested in more. And so are you."

True. Unfortunately. These past weeks had been torture. Wanting to see the Silverwing yet not daring to. Wanting to date yet refusing invitations. Wanting to feel the magic of his touch yet avoiding the fire.

"He's not like that," Debra insisted. "He's in training, and so am I."

Marilyn started to retort, but Debra spoke first. "Save your breath, Marilyn. You're going to need it up this grade."

With that, she gave out a burst of energy and sprinted ahead. Marilyn's protests spurred her on. That would teach her to keep bringing up Sterling's name.

"She only thinks of me as a friend." Sterling bemoaned the fact to his teammates after they finished ribbing him about seeing Debra that weekend.

Eddie laughed. "You got plans. Admit it."

Sterling threw a pillow across the motorhome at Eddie, who lay sprawled out on the couch. "There's no way I'm going to 'admit' anything, especially to you."

"You might as well make plans. You need to settle down. You're starting to act like an old man."

The other Silverwings in the motorhome hooted and hollered. Sterling let their comments slide by. He wouldn't dare let them know how close to the truth they were. He rolled his shoulders and rubbed a hand along his neck. His attitude and feelings lately did appear to reflect old age.

Cycling was becoming a daily struggle. The only time he felt spurred to perform was during a race. Yet this weekend he had placed lousy. His heart hadn't been in the competition because Debra hadn't been there to see him ride. Had his other wins this season been to impress her?

Sterling yearned for time alone. He needed to do some soul-searching and discover what was eating at him. Something was missing. That feeling usually meant he was on the wrong track. Serious thinking and earnest prayer usually straightened him out. Yet when he did have time alone, he couldn't focus. Debra was too much in his mind.

"Ever thought about what you're going to do when you're through cycling?" Sterling asked his teammates as he stood and began to pace the small area, in spite of the rocking motion of the motorhome.

His question sobered the other Silverwings.

"Are you serious? I barely think past the next race. You know me."

Everyone laughed at Eddie's comment but not wholeheartedly. The question was the kind they all faced but seldom talked about. They all loved racing. Leaving usually meant one thing—they *had* to quit.

Joe Carson came to Sterling's defense. "Eddie was just kidding about your being an old man."

Manuel Ortega spoke up from his place in the driver's seat. "Just because you're interested in a woman doesn't mean you have to give up racing. Look at me."

The men laughed. His comment broke the serious mood. Manuel had a woman in every state, new "fans" each season.

"You have enough relationships to make up for the whole team," Joe yelled. "We're trying to give Sterling serious advice. If he listened to you, he'd be in more trouble than he's in now."

"I'm not in trouble," Sterling insisted, sitting next to Joe when the Airstream swerved around a corner.

"When Sterling Wade doesn't have his mind on racing, he's in some kind of trouble."

"Relax, Wade. We're headed for Arizona. Debra's bound to be at *La Vuelta de Bisbee*."

Sterling's heart jumped a beat at the thought.

Eddie tossed back the pillow. "You'd better start thinking about the race and forget about Debra Valenzuela."

"He's right," Joe agreed. "That's one tough race."

"Don't you guys have enough to worry about yourselves? Just because I had a bad race the other day doesn't mean you have a chance this weekend."

"Listen to that confidence," Eddie jibed. "You'd think Wade was a real threat."

Sterling chuckled along with the men. "I've had enough of your humor at my expense," he told them. "I'm going in the back to lie down. Stay on the road, Ortega."

Before Manuel or the others could respond, Sterling headed toward the rear of the motorhome. He would be racing again, and he would see Debra. He needed to get his mind and emotions in alignment in order to do both.

Chapter Ten

Debra leaned her bike against the van and stared across the staging ground. Bisbee had died as a mining town years ago. Now the small community sported a thriving artist colony that, during the racing event, set up one of the county's biggest arts and crafts fairs.

The Arizona sunshine warmed the air, bringing the festival the ambience of spring. The fairgrounds rumbled with tourists, the area alive with the sounds of wind chimes and vendors hawking their wares. Excitement and tension hovered around the hub of the racing events.

Debra glanced at the silver motorhome for the tenth time that morning. She'd caught a glimpse of Sterling twice through a small window. She fiddled with her gears, lubed her chain, and peered at the big Airstream again.

Why wasn't he racing?

The men's race had started an hour ago. Cindy and the other women had gone to see them off. Debra stood on tiptoe to see over the crowd.

Should she go over to the motorhome? Maybe Sterling was sick. Or injured. She wanted to talk to him.

Forget Sterling. Focus on the race.

Debra tossed the can of chain lube into the back of the van and put one leg up on the bumper to tie her shoe. A movement out of the corner of her eye caught her attention.

Sterling jogged to her side and stopped, panting to catch his breath. "Planning to be today's star?"

Debra put her foot down and swung around to greet him. It

had been over two weeks since she'd last seen him. She smiled. "Thought maybe *you'd* be the star."

"You heard about Joe and Manuel? They were injured yesterday."

"I heard. You're okay, aren't you?"

He nodded, his blond hair stirring in the breeze.

To keep from staring, she leaned into the van and started organizing some of Ralph's tools. The smell of lubricants and oil assailed her heightened senses. "Why aren't you racing?"

"My foursome was disqualified because of the injuries, so I decided not to bother with the individual event."

Still holding a wrench, she straightened and watched him rub the back of his neck. "Is that wise?"

He eyed her from beneath his creased eyebrows, hesitated, and then took a deep breath. "I didn't race because I wanted to see you."

Avoiding his gaze, Debra twisted the wrench adjustment back and forth, then quickly leaned into the van and tossed the tool into its container. She picked up an Allen wrench. Sterling reached over, took the tool away from her, and set it aside.

He gently pulled her away from the van and with his free hand tilted her chin up.

She looked into his eyes.

Warm and caring.

"I've missed you."

"The schedule has been crazy." She could barely talk. "When the men are out racing, we're in. When the women are out, you're in."

She sounded like an idiot, but she couldn't concentrate, not with him standing so close and gazing into her eyes with that lazy smile.

He reached up and tucked a strand of hair behind her ear. "And there've been no parties yet."

She gave herself a small shake. "This is a tough race. We've all gone to bed early."

He sucked in his breath. "Do you know how much I want to hold you in my arms?"

Debra gulped, trying to ignore his clean soap smell. "The . . . the race."

"You start soon. That's why I'm letting you go."

Too late. Her legs wobbled and threatened to buckle. She backed up and let the bumper of the van support her.

He allowed the distance and stood with his hands braced on his hips. "I've been in the Airstream, trying to stay away. I prayed. I read. I did push-ups." He moved close again and stroked a finger down her cheek. "But nothing worked. I had to come see you."

His finger trembled. Her skin burned.

Papá. The race.

"You know how I feel about no involvements," she whispered.

He grabbed her hands and held them in his. "I know how *I* feel. I could easily love you, Debra."

Her chest constricted. Her fingers tightened around his.

He shook his head. "Don't say anything. I know you don't want a relationship, and I know why."

Debra bent her head and stared at his shoes.

He let go of her right hand and tilted her chin back up. "I understand. But I also know that you care about me."

She gasped. "I've never said anything to lead you on."

He chuckled. "Don't you think I can see your eyes light up when you see me? Don't you know that you touch my heart every time you smile?"

"Sterling, I—"

"Don't worry. I care too much about you to interfere with your dreams. I just want you to know that I *can* be a patient man. I'll wait as long as it takes." He smiled. "So go win your race today and this season. Go to Europe and become a famous star. But know this, Debra Valenzuela. I will be waiting for you."

"Sterling. It's not fair. I can't ask you to wait that long."

But she wanted to.

"It isn't a matter of fairness. It's simply a matter of what is. I can't help myself any more than you can."

She leaned back and looked into his eyes. She saw the desire that matched hers, the caring. She reached up and stroked his cheek, feeling the rough texture where he hadn't yet shaved. "Why did you come into my life now?"

He smiled and gently tugged her hair. "In spite of my baser inclinations—and yours—I'm going to help you get ready to race."

He stepped away, and a part of her went with him. She took a deep breath while he reached for her helmet and gloves from the back of the van. His fingers brushed hers when he gave them to her. Debra's hands shook.

Sterling walked to the side of the van and grabbed her bicycle. She looked past him and saw Hugh Ashford staring, a frown marring his features. Debra clenched her fists around her equipment. She nodded, but Ashford turned and walked away. He'd seen the two of them together.

She closed her eyes.

"Here's your steed. Need anything checked out?" Sterling stopped in front of her and studied her face. "What's wrong? You look like you've seen a ghost."

Words wouldn't come past her constricted throat. She nodded in the direction of Ashford's retreating back.

Sterling leaned over the bike and placed a hand on her shoulder.

Debra stepped back. "He keeps asking Ralph if we're involved."

Sterling gripped the handlebars of the bike. "I'll talk to him. I'll tell him that I won't be in the way."

Debra watched his knuckles whiten. She slapped her gloves against her thigh. Did she really want Sterling out of the way?

As if the matter was settled, Sterling handed her the bike. "How's your tire pressure?"

"Ralph gave the whole thing a good work-over. I lubed the chain before you got here." Thankfully her breathing returned to normal.

He leaned into the bumper of the van. "Have you been on the course? There are some tricky grades."

She hooked her helmet onto a handlebar and slipped the gloves on, wishing he would leave, glad he stayed. "You mean the climbs five miles out?"

"I should have known you'd have them identified."

"We were here last weekend working out."

Sterling sent her his most charming look. "So that's where you disappeared to. Ruined my weekend, you know."

She tested the gears and heard them click into place. "I heard you had some difficulty."

"I'm flattered you asked about me. Wish now I'd concentrated more on my racing. A win would've made a better impression."

"Don't race to impress me."

He laughed. "Didn't have your pretty smile to spur me on." He stood and stepped beside her, the bicycle between them. "Let me give you some tips on the road conditions."

The reminder of the race sobered her in spite of Sterling's nearness. "This race is critical. I have to win in order to get points for national placement," she admitted.

"If you ride like you have been, you'll be all right."

"I have to be better than 'all right.' There are three pro women's teams here. The competition is going to be cutthroat."

Sterling stepped back. "You have some team support now." He wanted to rub the tension from her brow and shoulders. "And you're clever. Look for every advantage, and take it."

She nodded and tucked her hair into her helmet. "I'll have to. Marilyn and the others will be there to support me at the beginning, but they'll have difficulty when it comes down to the wire."

"Don't start having doubts." Sterling knew that negative thinking could be one's downfall. "Keep picturing the win. You can do it."

"Thanks." Her smile warmed the expression in her dark eyes. "You're right."

"What would you do without me?"

She laughed. "And I keep telling you I don't need a hero."

"You shouldn't believe that. Besides, I'm going to be more than a hero. You know that, don't you?"

A flash of anxiety and longing flickered in her eyes. Sterling fought to keep from pulling her into his arms. Didn't she know that he would never hurt her? How could he, when he loved her?

Love.

Apprehension coursed through Sterling. How had it happened? He barely knew her. Yet he did. Enough to see the gentleness underneath the tough exterior.

"What are you afraid of, Debra? Why does commitment scare you?"

She looked away while she fiddled with the handlebars of her bike. "I have goals, Sterling. We discussed that before."

"Has it occurred to you that I could help you achieve them?"

"How? You don't even know what my needs are."

"I'm willing to listen and learn. Everything about you fascinates me. I want to know you."

"Don't do this to me." She frowned. "A cycle jockey can't give me what I need. I have to win. I have to become somebody important for . . ."

Sterling had sense enough to keep quiet, but seeing her obvious stress made him ache. Someone or something had hurt her somewhere along the line. He wished he could show her how special she was.

Cindy approached the van waving the white badge with the number 13 printed in large black letters. "Debra. You almost ready? I've got your number."

"Good grief. Couldn't you get another number?"

"I knew you'd be upset, so I tried. They wouldn't change it."

Debra backed her bike away from Cindy. "Thirteen is bad luck."

Sterling reached for the badge and stood behind Debra to pin it to her back. He could feel the tremors through her jersey. "There's no such thing as luck."

She twisted her head around to glare at him. "You don't call what happened to your teammates bad luck?"

"Accidents happen. Luck had nothing to do with it." He nudged her around so he could finish pinning on her number. "We don't always understand, but things have a way of working out for the best." He gave her a pat on the shoulder. "You're all set."

"I've got to go." Debra sounded tense and apprehensive.

Sterling watched as she and Cindy walked her bicycle toward the starting line. He wished he could truly be a knight in shining armor and make Debra's life perfect.

He had to let her go. She had to reach for her dreams. She would never be happy unless she gave it her all. Would he be able to wait that long? Sterling sighed. He would wait his whole lifetime if he had to. One thing he had realized for certain only a few minutes ago: he loved Debra Valenzuela.

And he wanted her for his wife.

While the women were on the road, Sterling meandered around the grounds. One of the sponsors, a Tucson radio station, had staged a band near the finish line. Music echoed across the grounds. Balloons decorated several booths selling bicycle merchandise. He spotted an interesting restaurant that featured health foods. Maybe he could talk Debra into going out to dinner.

At the end of the hour, Sterling headed for the finish line. He stood under the announcer's stage so he could hear the road reports.

"Number thirteen is in the lead," the announcer said into the microphone.

Sterling shoved his way toward the front of the spectators. Debra was pulling it off. He had to see this.

In the distance, two dots grew in size as a pair of cyclists made the final sprint. Kelly green and hot pink. Sterling knew it had to be Mary-Reva behind Debra.

He grinned.

"Go, Debra!"

Several shouts echoed as the cyclists neared the finish. Mary-Reva had pulled ahead, but Debra crept up to her wheel. Sterling knew she was going to make the final sprint.

Debra powered out. Just as she was about to pass, her wheel caught Mary-Reva's. The bicycle jerked and wrenched from Debra's grip, and suddenly she flew into the air. Kelly green crashed to the pavement.

The crowd groaned.

"No!" Sterling yelled, the sound drowning in a rush of terror. "Let her be okay." Sterling repeated the words over and over.

He pushed and shoved, forcing his way through the crowd that gathered to see. "Out of my way." Countless bodies blocked his path. Rage surfaced when he caught glimpses of Debra stretched out on the pavement.

"Debra, I'm coming!" he shouted. "Let me by. She needs me." His words were lost in the cacophony of voices.

"She's unconscious."

"Get the paramedics."

Sterling swallowed the metallic taste of fear. "Debra!" His whole body screamed with agony. He shoved aside a stranger bent over her inert form. Shivers of dread raced through him.

"I'm here, darling."

Sterling fought the hands that pulled at him.

Paramedics.

"Step back, sir."

Sterling stood. Fighting tears, he watched while the paramedics took Debra's vitals.

The ambulance forged its way through the mass of people. In minutes they had carefully moved her onto a stretcher and placed her in the emergency vehicle.

Sterling clenched and unclenched his fists as the siren

screamed away. "Don't take her from me now that I've found her," he murmured.

Debra dragged herself out of a black void. Pain shot through her. Gladly she slipped back into the inky depths.

"Debra!"

A familiar voice came from a great distance. She wanted to talk to him, but she couldn't form the words.

"Debra! Speak to me!"

Someone moaned, and she realized it was her own sob. She rose out of the void to blinding light. Pain gripped every nerve in her body.

The deep voice coaxed her closer. "Debra, darling. I'm right here."

Suddenly she knew she wasn't okay. Thrashing, she tried to sit up. Firm hands gently held her down.

"Easy now. Don't make any sudden moves. You're hurt."

Curtains hung on rods around her bed. Voices, shouts, and horrible moans filled the air. "Where am I?"

"Emergency room. The ambulance brought you."

A wave of fear washed through Debra. She had to get out of there. She struggled to rise.

"Stay still. Looks like a bad cut on your head and another on your side. Likely a concussion, maybe broken ribs."

She didn't care about her head and ribs. But she couldn't feel anything below her waist. "What's wrong with my legs?"

She looked at the needles and tubes. Panic set in.

"Sterling!" she gasped, and she reached for him.

He grasped her outstretched hand, but his eyes were somber. "I'm here."

She squeezed his fingers, absorbing the strength in his touch. "Don't leave me."

He rubbed his hand gently over hers. "Never."

His reassurance brought her comfort. His soothing voice and the warmth from the contact filled her with peace.

When she opened her eyes again, she didn't see Sterling. Distraught, she glanced around and noticed she had been moved from the ER to a private room. Her heart swelled when she saw him sitting near the foot of her bed.

"Sterling," she whispered.

He jumped up and came to her side. "Your legs are fine."

She grabbed his hand as if it were a lifeline. "I still don't have any feeling in them."

"Probably because of the ache in your shoulder and head."

As soon as he mentioned her shoulder, Debra winced. Her whole upper torso throbbed.

Sterling gave her ankle a slight tug. "Feel that?"

"Ow!" she yelled, though she was relieved to feel the pain. "What happened? One second I was gaining on Mary-Reva, and the next I was flying through the air."

"You must've hit a bump in the road or something, because your wheel caught on hers and brought you down."

"Is Mary-Reva okay?"

"She spun slightly but didn't lose control. She was far enough ahead of the others to win first place."

Debra moaned. "I needed that win."

"Stay quiet now. There will be other races."

The smells and sight of the sterile room stifled her. She tugged on Sterling's hand. "I want to leave."

Sterling gently pushed her back onto the pillows. He smoothed back her hair, which only frightened her more.

"The doctor will arrive soon to check up on you."

"Is Cindy here?"

"She and Ralph are in the waiting room. They would only let one of us at a time in here."

Debra groaned. "I knew I shouldn't have worn that number thirteen. It brought me the worst luck."

"I told you, there's no such thing as bad luck. That's super-stition," Sterling asserted. "What happened today was an accident. A mistake. Don't worry. Good will come out of it."

"Humph. What good could possibly come out of this? I'll be lucky if I can ever ride a bike again."

"Look, I realize cycling is important to you, but you still haven't spoken to the doctor. You don't even know the full extent of your injuries."

"I had a bad time learning to read and write in school. Studying was always so hard. I had to drop out of college. Now, when I finally have a chance to make something of myself that my father would be proud of, this happens."

Sterling closed his eyes, which annoyed Debra. She pulled her hand from his. "I don't need your help. What I do need is for the doctor to tell me I'll be able to ride again next weekend."

Debra tried to sit up, but the pain sent her senses reeling. Closing her eyes, she gave in to it.

Chapter Eleven

Sterling's heart ached for Debra, as a nurse checked her chart. The antiseptic smell of the hospital made his stomach churn. He'd had no idea that Debra harbored such inner pain. Disappointment or regret could eat at one's insides until there was nothing left but a shell. Sterling cared for Debra too much to let that happen to her.

A doctor came in, and Sterling was forced to leave. In the waiting room, he waved at Ralph and Cindy, who were sitting on a vinyl-upholstered couch, ignoring the blaring overhead television.

Ralph rose and hurried over to him. "What's the word?"

Sterling shook his head and rubbed the back of his stiff neck. "A dislocated shoulder, and they're keeping an eye on her in case of concussion."

"But all that blood?"

"A cut on her head that bled a lot but didn't really cause much damage." Sterling rotated his shoulders. "Does she have any family nearby we should call? She mentioned her father."

Cindy straightened her rumpled blouse and grabbed Ralph's hand. "She has family in California, but I'm not sure where or how to get in touch with them."

"You have the team to look out for. I'll stay with her until she can function on her own," Sterling said, before they could protest.

"She has roommates in Tempe," Cindy explained.

Sterling's stomach knotted. "A boyfriend?"

With empathy in her expression, Cindy assured him that they were young women who went to the university.

"College kids. I doubt they'd be much help."

Cindy settled into one of the vinyl chairs in the small room. "You're probably right. From comments Debra has made, they're pretty involved in their own activities and school, but they should at least know her parents' address."

Ralph sat in the other chair next to Cindy. "What about your cycling, Sterling? You can't be gone from the team too long."

"I'll resign if I have to." He was startled by his words. From the looks on Ralph and Cindy's faces, they were just as surprised. But it was the right thing for him to do. He sat in a chair across from them. "I can take her home when she's released."

Ralph raised a hand. "Let's not make any rash decisions. She may wish to stay with the team."

Sterling wanted to believe that. But he figured that the extent of her injuries would preclude that. He knew she'd be all right, though. Of that, he'd felt assured.

"Her shoulder's hurt, and while they think the head wound was superficial, there could be damage from a concussion." Images of her pale complexion kept swimming before his eyes. "They're running more tests. The doctor told me he would report to us as soon as he had more news."

Silence filled the room. They each waited with their own thoughts. Nurses in green scrubs scurried from room to room. A patient screamed. The sound sent chills down Sterling's spine. Fluorescent lights hummed, making him edgy and tense.

Sterling guessed that Ralph had to be as disappointed as Debra. She had drawn a lot of attention to the Desert Road-runners. Ralph wouldn't miss the glory as much as the excitement of being involved in the life of a winner. Moreover, Ralph and Cindy sincerely cared for Debra.

Sterling braced his elbows on his knees and held his head in his hands. What should he do? Did he really have a choice? There was nothing holding him to cycling anymore. The next step would be to open Debra's eyes and convince her that she needed him as much as he needed her.

Movement down the hall caught his attention. The doctor who had just evaluated Debra approached.

Sterling jumped up. "How is she?"

Ralph and Cindy were instantly beside him. "Will she be all right?"

"She'll be fine, but she suffered a concussion along with a dislocated shoulder."

Cindy groaned. "What about the bleeding from her head?"

"She suffered several scalp abrasions, none serious."

Sterling sighed with relief.

"We're going to observe her overnight. Then she should rest for a couple of days to be sure her concussion isn't major. Of course you realize she won't be able to ride for several weeks with that shoulder."

Cindy gasped. Ralph clenched his teeth. Sterling remained silent.

"She won't have to give up cycling altogether, will she?" Cindy asked, as she grabbed Ralph's arm for support.

The doctor smiled. "No. By next season she'll be back in great shape."

Sterling wondered how Debra was going to take that news.

"Next season!" Debra sat upright, grimacing at the pain shooting through her. "You can't be serious. Wait until next spring to race again? Impossible."

Sterling gently pushed her back down onto the pillows. "You're supposed to remain still until you recover from the concussion."

She glared at Sterling, who stood patiently at her side. She closed her eyes. He wasn't to blame. "What do doctors know? I'll be fine in no time. They'll see."

Sterling reached for the hand of her uninjured arm. "Miracles do happen. But for now you need to give your body a chance to heal."

Debra pushed her head into the pillow and moaned. "I was so close."

She yanked her fingers from his hand. "I'm really angry about this whole mess."

"That's a good sign."

She clenched her fist and pounded it on the bed. "Sterling. Please. This is serious."

Sterling lifted his hands in mock defense. "Anger spurs you on. Shows you're still fighting. Not giving up."

He smoothed his fingers across her forehead and continued in a soothing voice, "Things have a way of working out for the good, especially when you believe they will."

Debra stared at him. Did he honestly believe that? "This is 'good'? Look at me." She gestured toward her strapped-up arm, her bandaged head, and the room in general.

"I have enough faith for both of us."

She studied him for several long moments, noting the stubble of day-old beard. He'd stayed at the hospital all this time. She reached for his hand. His strength stemmed the tide of hopelessness engulfing her. "You'll need to. I don't have the conviction in me."

Sterling clasped both hands around hers. "I've witnessed many recoveries. Some of them amazing. I know you'll be another."

Debra settled into the pillows, exhausted and in pain. "I hope you're right."

"You'll see for yourself. With your determination and drive, you'll be indomitable once you recover. Not only in racing but in life."

At the sound of a knock, Debra glanced up to see Hugh Ashford at the door. She inwardly groaned when she read his expression.

"How are you doing?" Ashford asked, shifting uncomfortably at the foot of her hospital bed.

She straightened the sheet covering her. "Dislocated shoulder."

Ashford frowned. "Tough break. Sounds like you'll be out the rest of the season."

Sterling straightened and faced him. "Don't underestimate her. She'll miss several events. So take advantage of your opportunity to place, because by the time the Ore-Ida Challenge rolls around, Debra will be there."

Debra's eyes widened.

Sterling smiled confidently and winked at her.

Ashford grasped the curved metal foot of her bed. "I'll believe that when I see her roll up to the start." He made a fist and tapped the bed frame. "If you do make the Ore-Ida event, we'll talk about trying out for the team next season."

"And if I don't get there"—Debra grimaced as she hunched up in the bed—"can I still try out for the team next fall?"

"We'll see." Ashford shrugged, spun on his heels, and left the room.

Debra wanted to scream. "So close."

"You haven't lost out yet. A dislocated shoulder is not that big of a deal. After all, your legs are all right. You have that to be thankful for."

Debra scrunched her eyes shut. Images raged in her head. Yes, she was thankful about her legs, but what would she tell her father? Another failure? *No.* She refused. She opened her eyes. "Do you mean what you told Ashford? Can I get back into shape in time for the Ore-Ida Challenge?"

"I called my physical therapist back home. He said if you rest your shoulder and begin physical therapy, you might be able to build it back up in time for the championship, which is two months from now."

"That's the best news I've heard all day. Why didn't you tell me that in the first place?"

Sterling held up a hand. "Hold on now. It's no sure thing. A lot'll depend on you, such as, will you rest before you start therapy? You don't seem to be a very good patient."

She sank back into the pillows and laughed. "I'm the worst. But I can do anything if I have a goal to strive for."

"Thatta girl." Sterling enjoyed seeing the determination come back into her face. "Then I promise, you'll get back into shape. With my help."

Her brow creased in a questioning frown. "Your help? What do you mean?"

"You're going to need special coaching to get fully back into shape." He was almost certain she couldn't afford a professional therapist. "And who better than myself to work out with you? I've been through this same experience—five years ago during the European circuit, when I dislocated *my* shoulder. I know exactly what to do."

Her eyes looked like Apache-tear gemstones, dark and glittering. "But what about your team? Your races?"

"Let me worry about that. This is more important."

She studied him, looking for doubt or regret, but she didn't argue. Sterling let out the breath he was holding.

"When will Ralph and Cindy get back? I need to talk to them."

Sterling checked his watch. "Tex, Red, and the others are finishing up this afternoon. When they come in, Ralph said he'd drop by to pick you up. They'll be releasing you then."

He thought she'd be thrilled with that news, but Debra frowned. "Why aren't you racing?"

Sterling's heart skipped a beat. "I told you. You're more important to me than a race."

Still she frowned. "You shouldn't have passed up the event. You were placed in the top ten. You could have won today."

Sterling didn't pursue the matter. He had no intention of scaring her off with another declaration of his love.

"The local radio is covering the race. Would you like to hear what's happening?" he asked.

"I suppose I should cheer Tex and Red on."

Sterling chuckled as he fiddled with the remote control attached to her bed. "Go ahead and listen. You shouldn't be talking so much anyway."

"Would be my luck to have that doctor think I needed another day here."

Sterling sat on the lone chair in her room while they listened to the announcer give the details of the afternoon's event. When he heard Eddie Smith's name, he had a couple of pangs of remorse that he wasn't there. All he had to do was glance over at Debra, though, and the pangs disappeared.

By the time Ralph and Cindy arrived, Sterling had made up his mind to resign from the Silverwings and spend the next two months with Debra. He figured he could find a room nearby in Tempe. A university town always had plenty of rentals. The only difficulty would be in convincing her to accept his help. Would she go for the personal coaching?

Yes. She wanted to be back in the races.

It took two hours for him to gather his gear, notify his teammates, and to call his father, who was not surprised by Sterling's announcement—something Sterling would have to analyze later when he had the time. One of the Silverwings who always drove his own car took Sterling back to the hospital. When he arrived, the floor nurse gave him a note.

Dear Sterling,

Thank you so much for your generous offer, but I can't let you leave your team because of me. I would feel awful about such a sacrifice. I'm going to take your advice, though, and work my way back into condition. I appreciate all the moral support today.

Thanks again,
Debra

He crumpled the note in a tight fist. Closing his eyes, he scowled. Debra had a lot to learn if she thought a mere note was going to daunt Sterling Wade. He'd find her and show her what commitment meant.

Golden California poppies and blue lupine covered the hills as Debra strolled down the narrow San Joaquin Valley road. The gentle breeze tossed her hair about in wild disarray as the sun warmed the fields, filling the air with the combined fragrance of green grass and wildflowers. She'd forgotten how beautiful the spring plants were in California. She hadn't been home in April since she'd left for college. Today was a perfect day to enjoy the clear blue sky.

If only she were on her bicycle, this outing would be perfect. The country road would be an ideal place to ride. Carefully Debra moved her shoulder, still confined by a sling. Pain raced through her arm, although not as badly as it had a few days ago. The pangs helped deter the temptation to ride in spite of doctor's orders. And Sterling's.

Thinking of his instructions at the hospital brought back unwanted memories. The number of times the Silverwing came to mind disturbed Debra. There were entirely too many incidents. Like when she touched the strands of hair that he always tucked behind her ear. Like when she crawled into bed and thought of the way Sterling had so tenderly cared for her the day she was injured. Like when he'd talked about loving her.

Annoyed, Debra shook off the memories. She had no business thinking of Sterling Wade. She'd done the right thing to demand that Ralph and Cindy take off without him.

Oh, yes, she would have loved his help. She would have thrived on his care and attention. But she couldn't lead him on like that. She'd made the better choice. He deserved to be back on the road with his teammates.

A car horn beeped behind her. Debra stepped aside to let the vehicle pass but returned to the road when she saw it was her father's pickup. The green Chevy slowed to a stop.

"*Mija,* want a ride home?"

Debra smiled at the affection she saw in his eyes. She really should walk, but there were few times she could be alone with her father. "*Sí, Papá.* We need to talk." Reverting so easily to her first language always surprised her. The Spanish rolled effortlessly off her tongue.

"You look much better. The shoulder feeling good now?"

"*Sí.*" She hesitated and then took a deep breath. "I'm glad you and *Mamá* don't mind me spending this month at home."

"You're always welcome at home, *mija.* You know that." He put the truck into gear and started down the road. "This way I can introduce you to the young men around here. Maybe they might want to marry you."

"*Papá,* don't you dare bring up the subject with any of them. Young men these days don't want their marriages arranged."

"Nor women," he muttered.

She nodded, knowing it was difficult for her father when she was here. He didn't understand modern ways. He was from the old country.

She couldn't be angry with him. From his point of view, her life did seem precarious. There were none of the signs of success her brothers and sisters had. Her father equated their accomplishments with higher education. The signs of success he saw were the expensive cars, the beautiful homes, the things they could buy that he'd never had. She couldn't seem to make him understand that there were other worthwhile achievements in life.

"I'm serious about racing. There's no time for men." If there were, she'd be with Sterling right now.

"What meaning is there in racing a bicycle? You should be starting a family." He swerved around a corner.

Debra held on to the dash and chuckled. "Most parents are praying their daughters *don't* get pregnant."

"*¡Silencio!*" he ordered. "A young lady should not talk of such things. You know I mean marriage."

"Is marriage the only way you'll love me?" Debra sighed, tucking her hair back and thinking of Sterling.

Her father clenched the steering wheel. "I worry about you. You don't seem to have any goals. Any purpose."

"What do you think winning races takes? Goals! Purpose! And a lot more, like commitment and physical effort." How could he understand? She hadn't started riding until after she'd left home. He'd never seen the hours of workouts nor witnessed the commitment of time and energy.

"All that effort could be put toward something meaningful. Your brother is a doctor. He helps sick people. Your sister is a lawyer. She helps people with legal matters. Your—"

"Sports are meaningful. They provide good examples of hard work, skill, and teamwork, especially for youth. Don't you think that kids from the *barrio* might look at me and be inspired?"

"Not when you leave home all the time. How they going to know you're even from here?"

Debra clamped her mouth shut and clenched her fists in her lap. Riding with her father had been a mistake. Their discussions always ended up like this. Maybe she should return to Tempe. Her shoulder was much better now. She could manage.

When they pulled up to the house, Debra noticed a late-model sports car in the drive. "You expecting someone?" she asked, thinking it might be one of her brothers or sisters coming to her defense. They always did.

Just as she was about to step out of the truck, the screen door flew open, and a man came striding out, wearing a confident grin, his blond hair blowing in the breeze.

Debra gasped.

Sterling.

Chapter Twelve

Debra!" Sterling held his arms open wide. "It took me forever to find you."

"How did you? Why?" Joy, embarrassment, and anger all vied to explode from her. She wanted to run and hide. She wanted to tell him to go back to his team. She wanted to run into his embrace.

"Debra!" *Mamá* exclaimed, following Sterling out the door. "That is no way to greet guests."

"Mamá!" Debra protested.

One look at the expression on Sterling's face, and she felt remorse for her cold greeting. She walked over to him and, mindful of her parents watching, gave him a slight, one-armed hug, enough to catch the spicy scent of him, to feel his day's growth of beard on her cheek, and to see the caring in his eyes. "I'm sorry. You surprised me, that's all."

"Remind me never to surprise you again." He grabbed her hand and gave it a squeeze before turning toward her mother. *"Está bien,* Señora Valenzuela. Debra knows that seeing me means tough workouts for her. *¿Qué no, querida?"* he said in fluent Spanish.

So that was how he'd wrangled an easy invitation—speaking Spanish won points with both her parents. And how had he discovered her home?

He traced a finger along her sling. He hadn't touched her arm, but her skin still tingled as if he had. "How's the shoulder?"

"It's sore." She let go of his hand and backed away. She studied him, wanting to imprint everything about his features

108

into her brain. She looked into his silver-gray eyes that now locked with hers.

She took a deep breath and broke the look. Turning to her father, she spoke in Spanish. "He's a friend. I met Sterling at the meets. He races bicycles."

The grin on her father's face disappeared. *Papá* wouldn't be so easy to impress. A professional cyclist was not high on his list of prospective partners for Debra.

"Is that all you do?" her father asked in his accented English.

"I'm in business with my father."

That news brought back the smile. "Welcome to my home. *Mi casa es su casa.*" He offered the traditional Mexican salutation.

"It's a pleasure to meet Debra's parents. Quite a daughter you have there. I bet you're really proud."

Debra tensed.

Papá's smile disappeared again.

Sterling quirked an eyebrow, obviously perplexed.

Debra's mother quickly bailed him out. "She's a wonderful daughter, our youngest, Señor Wade."

"Sterling, please."

Debra stood by helplessly, watching Sterling charm his way into her parents' hearts. Not a difficult task, given the generous nature of the Valenzuelas.

"I was just asking your *mamá* if there was a place nearby where I could stay."

Debra refused to indulge them by speaking Spanish. "You need to go back to your team." Even though she was happy to see him, she couldn't ask him to make that kind of sacrifice.

"I'm here to work out with you. We have an extensive schedule to follow in order to get you back into shape before the Ore-Ida Challenge," he continued in Spanish.

" 'We'?" Debra fisted her good hand on her hip. "Where is this *we* coming from?"

Her mother sang out in lilting Spanish. "You're here to help our Debra? *Qué bueno.*" She raised her arms to the heavens. "In that case, you must stay here at the house."

"*¡Mamá!*" Panic forced Debra to revert to Spanish. "He can't do that."

Sterling beamed. "How generous and kind of you, Señora Valenzuela. But please, I couldn't impose."

"But I insist. Isn't that right, Debra? It wouldn't be any trouble at all. I miss my sons. It would be nice to have a young man around the house again."

"Humph," her father muttered as he crossed his arms and frowned at Debra.

Sterling accepted the offer, then cast Debra a mischievous grin. "Seemed easier to give in," he leaned close and whispered, his breath tickling her ear. "Besides, there didn't look like much in the way of accommodations in town."

True, the small central valley town's one old run-down motel made the places Ralph and Cindy picked out look like a Hilton.

"I suppose you can spend the night," Debra conceded as she brushed back her hair and settled her hand in the crook of her neck, "but you have to leave in the morning."

"Don't pay Debra any mind." Her mother waved a hand. "Stay as long as you want."

Sterling shrugged in mock helplessness, placed his hand at Debra's back, and walked her through the screened-in porch.

Great. How was she going to have the strength to send Sterling back to his team if he kept her senses spinning?

The door slammed behind her father as he followed them. "Are you her coach or trainer?" he demanded suspiciously.

Debra frowned. "No."

Sterling grinned. "Yes."

"I told you, he's just a friend. He's supposed to be riding with the Silverwings." Debra pulled away from Sterling's touch. "Where are they racing this weekend? At the Visalia Classic, kicking off the California Classic?"

"I'm not keeping track. I told you in Bisbee that I was going to leave the team and help you recover and train." He rubbed his jaw in frustration. "I've spent the last week trying to find you."

It couldn't have been easy, since she hadn't told anyone in Arizona her home address. Not even Ralph and Cindy knew where she was from. "And how *did* you manage to find me?"

"Your roommates helped out. They went through your papers and found a California address. Sorry about that."

Debra didn't know whether to be annoyed or flattered at all the trouble he'd gone to.

"I flew out here and met your brother, Carlos." Sterling leaned against the large table they used for outdoor meals on the screened porch.

Her father caught up to them. "You spoke to Carlos?" When Sterling nodded, her father grinned. "How is my son?"

"Told me to tell you that he'll be coming down for the weekend."

"You'd better take Alfonso's room. Alfonso is our second son," *Mamá* explained. "He won't mind that you use his room." Her mother opened the front door and ushered them inside.

Cluttered and smelling of garlic and corn tortillas, the house showed years of use. Worn furniture filled the small room that had been paneled in the early seventies when dark woods and shag rugs were popular. Old-fashioned doilies, yellowed by age, covered the threadbare arms of the couch and chairs. Photos covered the walls and shelves. Sports trophies and handmade knick-knacks abounded. Most of the items were ancient history, but her mother refused to throw them out.

Mortified, Debra wondered what Sterling thought of her family's modest home.

As if reading her thoughts, he commented, "I like your place. It's homey and comfortable."

She herself loved the cozy feeling and the flood of memories that the room always generated, but she'd never brought anyone home before. Nor had her brothers and sisters, for that matter.

"We weren't expecting company," Debra began to apologize.

Sterling pulled Debra beside him as he settled on the plaid couch. "Don't go to any bother. I like spontaneous visitors myself. Then they have to take me the way I am."

Her father agreed, as he seated her mother in her chair and then sat in his favorite recliner across from the couch. Debra stared at her parents, who were obviously quickly warming up to Sterling. The Silverwing had charm—she had to give him credit for that. Hadn't he charmed his way into *her* heart?

Papá leaned back in the recliner. His pose looked casual, but Debra saw his rapt attention on Sterling. "So you come here to help my Debra. Maybe you can talk some sense into her. She should be back in school."

"Not everyone is cut out for university," Sterling surprised her by saying. He crossed an ankle on top of his opposite knee and reassuringly patted her hand. "Everyone has their own needs and desires."

"*Sí.* She is smart. She could do as well as her brothers and sisters if she tried."

Debra jumped to her feet. "How about some lemonade?"

Her father's continual criticism grated on her, and Sterling didn't need to hear the disapproval. Her ploy to change the subject didn't work, however. She could hear her father carrying on about how wonderful her sisters, Maria and Anna, were.

Debra struggled to get ice with her good hand, then hurried to pour the lemonade, wishing she hadn't left Sterling alone with her parents.

Sterling cast her an empathetic smile when she handed him a chilled glass.

"I'm sorry," she mouthed silently.

He shook his head, indicating she shouldn't be. A lot of good that did. They both had to continue listening.

"Debra is the youngest. We spoil her too much."

Debra returned to her place on the couch. "Now, *Papá,* don't bore Sterling with the whole family history." He'd already been regaled about how great her brothers and sisters were, but he didn't need to hear all of Debra's shortcomings.

On second thought, maybe if he knew them, he'd change his mind about staying.

After an hour, her father finally ran out of conversation. Debra helped her mother pick up the glasses and then led Sterling outside.

"You can park your car in the garage in the back. My brothers liked to work on their cars. I think my father mainly built it so he could keep an eye on them and make sure they weren't getting into trouble with the other boys in the *barrio*."

Sterling chuckled as he followed her across the lawn. "My father kept me on the bicycle. I'm sure for the same reason."

Debra paused in front of the garage and watched Sterling's expression. "*Papá*'s plan worked for my brothers. Did your father's work for you?" She longed to know everything about Sterling—his childhood, his family, his likes and dislikes.

"Good thing for you I stayed out of trouble. Heroes can't have spotted records." Sterling shoved open the heavy garage door and stepped inside. Debra followed and chewed on a thumbnail as he took in the large room.

Shelves cluttered with tools lined one wall. A large open space stood empty now but had once been filled with cars. In the center sat an old woodstove, used to heat the shop during the cold days of winter. She could remember the tang of burning wood scenting the yard. Now the smells of grease, oil, and gasoline assaulted her senses.

Sterling's muscles flexed as he latched the door. He spun around, arms wide and genuine appreciation expressed in his gray eyes. "Wow. This is a man's dream."

Debra watched him study the array of tools. "Do you like working on cars?"

"Not really, but I could learn if I spent time in here." He circled in front of her and winked. "Now bicycles—that's another story."

Debra looked at the room, trying to figure out what about it appealed so much to the male of the species. Not only had her brothers spent their youth in here, but most of the neighborhood boys hung out with them here too.

Sterling walked around, inspecting the lighting and the space. "This is perfect. Does your dad use this now?"

She pointed toward the side of the garage that contained the most clutter. "Just that corner, when he has to work on his or *Mamá*'s car."

"This would make a great place for you to work out. We could set up a gym in here."

Debra stared in amazement. Couldn't the man see that the Valenzuelas didn't have the means to buy gym equipment?

He continued. "I can have my equipment shipped here. We don't need much. Some simple weights, my cross-country glider, a turbo-trainer, a stationary bike, and a roller trainer."

Debra lifted her good hand. "Wait a minute. You can't just order up all of that stuff. It'd cost a fortune to ship that heavy—"

"It won't cost me a thing. My dad's trucks come up and down Highway 99 every day. I'll just have him load up my gear, and his driver will drop it off on his way to another delivery."

Sterling was evidently taking his knight-in-shining-armor role seriously. A seed of hope began to sprout. "You're sure there wouldn't be any charge for moving all that stuff?"

Sterling moved close and tucked a strand of her hair behind her ear. "One of the advantages of being the son of the boss. We could have everything we need in two days. If we start training now, you'll be in great shape for the Ore-Ida Challenge. What do you say?"

Debra shivered. This was too good to be true. There had to be a catch somewhere. Her eyes locked with his. "If I say yes, my commitment will only be for the training. I'm not promising anything to you personally."

She studied his features but saw no clue to his emotions. Grabbing his hand, she spoke. "I haven't changed my mind. I don't want any involvements, Sterling. You of all people should know why."

"I understand perfectly." Sincerity gleamed in his silver-gray eyes. "There's nothing more tragic than seeing someone give up on their dreams. I understand where your father is coming from, but you need to fulfill your own goals. I can help you do that."

How she wanted him to. She wanted him to stay with her forever. But it wasn't fair to ask him. "Why would you?"

"Because I love you."

Heat crept up her neck to her face. She started to protest, but before she could utter a word, Sterling put a hand to her lips.

"I know, I know. You don't love me. *Yet.*" His eyes sparked with mischief as he tucked the errant strand of hair behind her ear. "I told you before, I can be a very patient man. I can wait until you do all the things you feel you have to before you're ready to commit."

His touch hypnotized her. Finally she managed a hoarse whisper. "But what if it takes me my whole lifetime to accomplish all I want?"

"Then I'll be by your side, cheering you on."

She wanted to forget her father. Forget her dreams. Just live for the moment. Would it be fair to Sterling? "What if I never . . . love you?"

A flicker of sadness crept into his eyes. "That's a risk I'm willing to take." His smile returned. "But I don't think I need to worry about that."

She wanted to believe him. "How can you be so sure?"

Sterling slid his fingers down her arm and took her good hand in both of his. "It's a knowing, Debra. I love you very much. Don't ask me why. I've just felt it in my heart from the first time I met you."

She gripped his fingers. "You're scaring me."

He stood perfectly still. "Don't ever be afraid of me. I won't rush or pressure you. Take as much time as you need. Ask me anything you want. Just don't close your heart to me." He played with a lock of her hair. "Give us a chance."

Drawn by his touch and the sensitive tone of his voice, Debra took a deep breath. "I don't know what to say."

"How about, 'Yes, Sterling. Send for your equipment, and let's get me into shape.'"

Debra had to laugh at that practicality coming on the heels of the deepest declaration she'd ever heard. "I don't know why I'm doing this. That bump on the head must've been more serious than I thought. But—" She paused, knowing that her decision would change things between them. Should she decide something so important when her heart was turning to mush? "Yes. Go ahead and send for your equipment."

He leaned toward her, and Debra thought he would kiss her. He paused. She remained still, half hoping he would make the move, yet knowing they needed to stay on a professional basis.

His breath fanned her cheek. "I'm an emotional guy, so get used to it."

That was the problem. Debra worried that she was going to get used to entirely too much. *Concentrate on the Ore-Ida Challenge.* That was her only defense.

Once the decision had been made, Sterling had Debra find buckets, brushes, and cleanser so he could start on their project. Debra returned to the house to help her mother, while he went to work scrubbing the floor greased up from years of working on cars. In the cleanest corner he found some cheap indoor-outdoor carpeting and covered a space where Debra could do floor exercises.

Three hours later and more than pleased, Sterling gazed around the transformed garage. They had a private place to work out, one that afforded plenty of space. Now all that remained was to establish a suitable routine and get Debra into shape.

"Is this the same place?" Debra stood at the door with two plates filled with tortas and veggie sticks stacked on top of each other.

"Ah. Just in time to admire my handiwork."

She held out the plates and gestured for him to take one and follow her outside to sit on the green grass for a picnic.

Sterling helped her sit and joined her.

Debra spoke in a quiet voice. "One thing about you, Sterling. Once you set your mind to something, watch out, because it's done before you can blink an eye."

"One of my better traits." He stretched out on the cool grass and inhaled the fresh-cut scent. He hadn't been that sure earlier. She'd caught him off-guard with her apparent reluctance to accept his help, before she finally acquiesced and agreed to his staying.

"I'm so glad you're modest," she teased, before she took a bite of her torta, working her tongue to keep the avocado from squishing out the sides of the roll.

Sterling winked, enjoying the sight of her bare legs crossed, her makeup-free olive skin, and her hair tossed about her shoulders. Sterling savored the shredded beef, tomato, lettuce, and avocado.

Debra set her food aside. "After all that work cleaning, I bet you're wishing you were back with your team."

He paused, about to take another bite. "Are you kidding? I haven't felt this good in months. For the first time this season, I feel like I actually accomplished something worthwhile." The statement surprised Sterling as much as it did Debra. Ever since he'd decided to work with Debra, the emptiness and longing had disappeared. He smiled as he bit down on the torta.

Debra studied him with her dark eyes. He let her see the peace that he felt as he stretched his legs out and braced his body on one elbow. He put the plate down in front of him and nibbled on the veggie sticks.

"Later this afternoon we'll start you on a routine of floor exercises. You can work on those until the equipment arrives."

"That's a good idea. My muscles already feel sluggish."

"You won't think so once we get started." Sterling chuckled as he put the last of the torta into his mouth.

A few hours later his words proved true. Debra walked toward him doing deep knee lunges.

"Lengthen your stride," he advised as he stood on the edge of the improvised floor mat. "The stretch will strengthen your upper leg muscles."

She placed her right foot mere inches in front of his wide stance and pulled herself upright, placing her face directly in front of his. Her eyes locked in a challenging glare. "You're supposed to be my hero, not my slave driver."

Sterling held his ground, grinning. "This is nothing. Wait until the equipment gets here."

Debra groaned.

Sterling resisted the urge to brush back her hair. He took a deep breath, enjoying her scent mingled with the oily smells of the garage. He wanted so to kiss her.

"You'll thank me when you step up to the starting line in Boise."

"Humph." She pivoted on the ball of her left foot and lunged away from him.

The next morning they continued Debra's schedule. Her body condition and her youth would be to her advantage. "Since your legs weren't injured, you'll be able to keep them in shape with the trainers. As soon as your arm is out of the sling, you can begin on the glider and soon after on the stationary bike."

Perspiration streaked down the sides of her face and onto her neck. "Are they scheduled to arrive today?"

He handed her a towel. "Any time. Try a series of side kicks."

Before Debra finished a second set of side kicks, her father entered the garage. She faltered as the older man perused the large room, a scowl marring his sun-worn features.

"A waste of time," he muttered.

"She'll make better progress when the exercise equipment arrives," Sterling said, beginning to understand why Debra had such a need to please her father.

"Your truck driver just called. Said he'd be here in a few minutes." His Spanish echoed in the silent room.

"Good. I want to set up the gym this afternoon."

Debra's father rubbed his work-worn hands on his jeans. "I'll help."

Sterling nodded, glad for the opportunity to get to know the older man.

Sterling turned to Debra. "Take a break, and get some lunch if you want."

"I'm outta here." Debra grabbed her towel and jogged out the door.

Was she running from the workout or her father? Probably both.

Debra was in town, grocery shopping with her mother, when the large semi pulled into the spacious yard with a hiss of air brakes and a blast of the horn. While the diesel engine idled, Sterling hurried to help unload the large pieces of equipment.

"Let us do that, Mr. Wade. We've got a forklift in here."

Sterling noticed that Debra's father looked impressed with the deference and respect of the drivers. *Good.* Anything to help his cause.

He pointed out the sites for each piece of exercise equipment. Fortunately most of them were still assembled. "Set the turbo trainer in that corner." After the last box was unloaded, the truck rolled out of the driveway, sporting the Coronado Industries logo on its sides.

Debra's father strode over to Sterling, his shoulders back and his head held high. "I see those trucks all the time. Your father owns that company?"

Nodding, Sterling pushed and shoved the stationary bicycle into place. "We're partners."

The senior Valenzuela whistled in surprise. "You must be a big company to own a truck like that."

"We have a fleet of twenty."

"And he doesn't object to you riding bikes instead of working?"

"I do work. He runs the company six months in the spring and summer while I race. In the fall and winter he plays golf while I take care of business."

The older man rubbed his face and slapped on his worn western hat. "I don't understand why you and Debra want to ride bikes."

"Hopefully you'll find out while we're here."

Tantalizing aromas of homemade corn tortillas and beans drifted from the house. Debra entered the kitchen, the screen door banging behind her.

She stepped over to the counter and grabbed a hot tortilla before her mother could swat her hand away. "Smells yummy. Can I help with lunch?"

"You can help by not eating all of it before I set the table." Her mother's Spanish rolled across her tongue.

"I've worked up an appetite." Debra reached for another tortilla when her mother turned her attention back to the hot griddle.

"You work hard out there."

"I have to stay in shape so I can race again."

Her mother's shoulders sagged with the weight of her doubts. "Your father worries—"

"So what else is new? I've done everything I can think of to make him understand what I do."

Another tortilla sizzled on the hot grill, scenting the air with corn *masa*. "Maybe Sterling will help convince him."

Debra pulled aside the chintz curtain at the window behind the kitchen sink to catch a glimpse of Sterling as he shoved the cross-country glider into the garage. She sighed. How could she stay on a friendly basis with him when her heart thudded from the mere sight of him? She dropped the curtain and turned to her mother.

"He'll have Sterling convinced I'm a *burro* before the month is out."

Mamá remained silent as she patted a ball of *masa* into another tortilla. Debra peeked out the window again and saw her father lift a heavy box and hand it to Sterling.

She gripped the soft material. "Why does *Papá* hate me?"

"Your father loves you, *mija*. He blames himself because you don't stay in school."

"Yeah. Right." Debra turned and with her good hand began pulling plates out of the cupboard. She plopped them down onto the counter with a clatter and tossed napkins and spoons onto the top plate.

"You break a dish, and you buy me a new one."

Debra eyed her short, stocky mother. Taking a deep breath, she carefully picked up the plates and took them over to the large Formica table.

Debra glanced out the window again. "I'm glad they're getting along."

"He's a nice young man. He's in love with you."

The spoons slid out of Debra's fingers onto the table. "He told me." She turned pleading eyes to her mother. "What am I going to do? I can't get involved with anyone right now."

Her mother piled several more cooked tortillas onto a plate. Debra's stomach growled.

"Seems to me you already are."

Debra choked. "He's just a friend. Nothing more."

"Your father would be satisfied if you were married, especially to a man like Sterling."

"I'm not marrying to please *Papá*. I want him to be proud of *me,* not who I married."

"You make sure your intentions are clear." Her mother's

Spanish lilt filled the kitchen. "Don't lead Sterling on. He's an honorable young man."

Debra straightened from placing the napkins around the table and stared at her mother. "I do believe you'd plead Sterling's cause over mine."

Her mother shrugged and patted another tortilla.

Chapter Thirteen

Sterling watched Debra closely, gauging her strength and stamina. Sweat darkened her T-shirt and trickled down her neck and shoulders. Her muscles rippled under the damp skin. These past three weeks she'd worked hard and steadily. Now that her arm was out of the sling, he could push her more.

"That's good. Keep up that pace for another ten minutes," he advised, stepping in front of the turbo trainer.

Debra groaned as she pedaled harder. "You make Ralph's training seem like grade school."

"Hardly. It just feels more difficult because you're pulling yourself back into shape. When you were working out with Ralph, you were already built up."

Debra's legs flexed as she continued her pedaling. "I can't believe how much strength you lose in just a few weeks."

"Look at what you've gained in that time. See what persistence accomplishes? Visualizing the outcome?"

Pausing in midstroke, Debra studied him for several seconds. "You really do take all this visualization-meditation stuff seriously, don't you?"

"It's the most important part of my success. By building on it, I can face anything."

For endless seconds she watched him closely. Sterling forced himself to remain quiet so that the seed he'd just planted could take hold.

Just as suddenly as she'd stopped, she started pedaling again. Sterling gripped her handlebars and looked her square in the eyes. "We're both benefiting from this experience. You're getting back into shape."

Debra's glance locked with his. "And what are you getting?"

Sterling leaned forward and smiled. "As I mentioned before, you're building my enthusiasm and helping me set new goals."

She lowered her head and pedaled faster. "Seems like a poor trade."

Sterling chuckled, knowing she'd had enough for the day. "Time for a break."

"Relief for the wicked," she muttered, yet she slowed her pace.

"This is why you need me. You overextend yourself."

"The knight-in-shining-armor bit again?" She smiled but stopped pedaling and grabbed the water bottle he handed her.

"Aren't you glad I'm here?" Sterling knew she wouldn't tell him what he really wanted to hear. Nevertheless, he fished for any compliment he could get. The guys would have a field day if they could see the state he was in. They'd always warned him that when he fell in love, the landing was going to be hard. They'd been right.

Debra gave him the empty bottle, took the towel, and wiped her face and neck. "What I can't figure out is how you've managed to entwine my parents around your little finger."

His growing relationship was no mystery to Sterling. "Love, *querida*. It works every time."

She slid off the trainer and walked stiffly to a nearby table. "I bet you had a lot of love in your family. You probably grew up in a nice upper-class neighborhood and had everything you ever wanted."

"Yes to both, but don't think that doesn't come with its own set of problems." Sterling followed her and held her arm as she stood on one leg and lifted the other onto the table.

She bent forward and stretched. "You're a very loving and caring person, Sterling. That's something you learn from family."

"There's no way you can put a value or measure on the love

and companionship that you have within your family. Your brothers and sisters adore you. Your parents are strict, but that's because of love. They want the best for you."

She glanced at him. "You missed not having brothers and sisters, didn't you?"

He saw caring in her eyes. "I used to fantasize about a family like yours."

"That explains a lot," she murmured as she lowered her leg and stretched the other on the table.

"Not that I don't love my own parents. They're wonderful. Wait 'til you meet them."

"Will I meet them? Do they come to any of the races?"

He chuckled at her eagerness. He was pleased to see that she was interested in knowing his family just as much as he was interested in knowing hers. It proved what he was beginning to suspect: she was in love with him.

"You've done well today. Let's go sit outside and rest before you start the next round."

Debra followed him out the door. "What was it like for you as a child?"

"We traveled a lot. That's probably why we're so close. Since we were places where I didn't know any other kids, I spent most of my time with my parents."

"What made you start racing?"

"We went to Europe for my sixteenth birthday. I saw my first race in France. All that excitement and watching those cyclists struggle across the finish line hooked me." He held her hand while she lowered herself onto the cool grass. He sat beside her. "We went to Madrid next, and I talked my parents into renting a bicycle while Dad was in meetings. I haven't stopped riding since."

"That's true dedication."

"I think my dad was relieved that I found something to keep me out of trouble."

Her quiet laughter wrapped around him like a touch of velvet. "Did you really manage to stay out of mischief?"

He nodded but didn't tell her that his father started a cycling club and began sponsoring the events so his son could compete. By the time Sterling hit college, he'd convinced his father to bring one of the top European bicycle designers to the States. That was the start of Silverwings, Inc., and next came the team.

Sterling had been behind the scenes in the development of the whole enterprise. It had been exciting at the time, but now he needed something deeper, more meaningful—like Debra. A family.

"How's your shoulder doing?"

"Sore but nothing to worry about. Did you start racing right away?"

He grinned. "I always go after what I want."

"I do believe that."

He remained still for long seconds, staring into her eyes. *Trust me.* "I never forced my way."

She sat, eyes locked with his, processing his words, then stretched flat on her back in the lush grass.

Sterling didn't realize he'd been holding his breath. He released it slowly and sat very still. Neither spoke. Sterling didn't mind; she'd just shown him that she trusted him, and it pleased him how unquestioning of his advice she had become. In the realm of her bicycling, she had given over her life to his care. Perhaps if he could prove to her how much he would treasure that responsibility, she would trust him with her heart.

Perspiration poured off Debra as she pushed herself beyond her limit. She shouldn't be straining like this, but she preferred it to sitting around with time to contemplate. Debra stopped cycling and lowered her head to her folded arm, which rested across the handlebars. Life seemed suddenly muddled. Her goals had been clear. Her life planned out. Now . . .

Sterling! All she could think about was the Silverwing. She sighed. If she didn't know better, she'd say she was in love.

Debra straightened immediately. *Love? Never.* She was imagining emotions that weren't there. *Thankful. Appreciative.* Those were the words to use. She was forming a crush similar to those patients developed for their doctors. She'd had a serious setback. Sterling was helping her climb out of it. *Overly grateful.* That explained this disturbing preoccupation with the Silverwing.

Not the fact that her family adored him. Not the sight of him that sent her senses scattering. Not the smiles that could melt her heart. *A crush.* That's all it was. As soon as she was back on the circuit, she would forget all about Sterling.

Who was she kidding? She *was* in love. Up to her knees, elbows, head over heels in love.

Debra resumed pumping the turbo trainer. Welcoming the distracting pain in her muscles, she moved faster.

The door to the garage opened.

"You're going to cramp up if you keep going like that." Sterling's voice cut into her thoughts and soothed the ragged edges of her nerves.

Debra slowed and gasped for breath. "I'm under control."

He studied her features as he walked in front of her. "Are you?"

Knowing how well he could read her thoughts, she covered her face with the towel that had been draped around her neck.

"Something bothering you?"

"Just out of breath," she lied.

His fingers clasped the towel and gently tugged. "Debra, look at me."

Slowly, she raised her head and did not make an effort to hide the turmoil within. *Let him see the confusion and the doubts.* "You know what's bothering me."

"No, *querida.* Don't do this to us."

A tear streaked down her cheek. "I don't know what I feel anymore. I used to be so sure."

"It's the accident. That's all. When you're back in top shape, your emotions will stabilize."

"I'm not sure I want them to," she admitted. "Being with you seems so right. Yet I know I have to carry on with this training."

He grasped her hands. Debra clung to their warmth and strength as if to a lifeline. "Being with me *is* right. Continuing your training *is* right. You're trying to put logic into what your heart feels. That's why you feel disoriented. What you need is to bring your heart into your mind." He brushed away her tear with a corner of her towel.

She looked deeply into his eyes, searching for the truth he always seemed to have at his fingertips. "I don't understand."

His smile warmed the chill inside. He guided her off the trainer and began walking with her around the room. "Tell me what you don't understand."

"How do you know all these things? How can you be so patient?"

"I've lived my dream. I've accomplished what I wanted to in racing. So I'm ready for other things." He paused and pulled her around to face him. "You are just beginning. You must follow your own dreams. I understand that."

"I know. Basically, that's what I have been doing."

"So what's the problem?"

Her heart heavy and aching, Debra stared out the window at the blossoms on the peach tree. The crisp colors were silhouetted against the blue sky. If life could be clear-cut, she wouldn't feel so disoriented and miserable.

"What is it you truly desire? That is what you need to focus on."

"I thought I was racing to earn my father's respect. Now that I've had this setback, he won't even have the satisfaction of seeing me win any races."

"Do you honestly think placing first is going to earn his love and respect?"

"He'd have *something* to brag about. My brothers and sisters have their degrees, their careers. I couldn't give him that, so I wanted to hand him fame."

"Fame does not bring a reward. The reward is the feeling inside that you did everything you could to achieve it." Sterling paused and shook his head. "It's the knowing that you applied yourself to the fullest. It's the satisfaction that you brought yourself to the peak. That is the reward."

Debra's brow furrowed in puzzlement. "Sure it is for me, but what about my father?"

"There is no satisfaction in seeking approval from man. Contentment comes from within you." He continued walking. "Discover who you really are, and you won't have to worry about your parents' love and respect."

She stiffened but followed him. "I don't understand what you mean."

"Your peace and contentment will rub off onto others. You don't need a trophy to buy respect. You earn it by proving you can meet life head-on and handle it."

Debra halted midstride.

Sterling turned to face her. "You've had a major setback. You could have given up and gone around moping and complaining. But no, you dug in your heels and are striving to recover. That effort will win more respect and love than any first-place award."

Sterling meant what he said. She could read admiration and love in his eyes.

"I haven't accomplished anything yet."

"Not true. You raised Ralph and Cindy's level of expectations. You brought Marilyn and other women together as part of a winning team. You've inspired Tex and Red to push on to their limit."

He lightly ran his fingers up and down her arms. "Most of all, you've helped me find new purpose. Redirect my goals."

Can it be true? She wanted to believe him, but logic kept rearing its ugly head. Sterling was too strong and grounded to be filled with so much self-doubt. "I couldn't have possibly done that."

He grasped her hand, his fingers warm. "When we met, I was burned out, bored, listless. Your enthusiasm and drive to win is rubbing off on me. It's like you're giving me a zap of new energy."

"You should be back with your team." She knew her words were true, yet she really wanted him to stay.

"I'm in the right place at the right time. You need me, and I need you." He gave her fingers a squeeze, let go of her hand, and continued walking her around the room. "And my advice is to talk to your father."

She stared at him. Perhaps he was right. "I'll try talking to him. How did you get so wise?"

"Going through trials like you are now."

"I may be younger than you, but believe me, I've had my share of trials before now too."

"Everyone has them."

Debra envied Sterling his peace and faith, but she wasn't sure she wanted to open up and reach for them herself. There were too many doubts.

Debra sighed and pulled away from Sterling. Maybe he was right all along, and it was a good thing that she had been injured and had returned home. Her father could see how much work was involved in her sport. And getting to know Sterling was proving to be beneficial toward her well-being in more ways than just her physical health. The world looked different when she was around him, brighter and full of hope.

"Let's go inside and have breakfast," Sterling suggested. "I saw your mother fixing pancakes."

Debra laughed. "First things first. Food for the body. Then I'll try some food for the soul."

Sterling followed her inside the house. Maple syrup and a large platter of bacon scented the small room. *Mamá* stood at the stove pouring whole-wheat batter onto the hot griddle.

Her father sat at the table, sipping a cup of coffee. "Sit down and join us." He gestured toward the empty seats.

Sterling held out a chair for Debra, but she shook her head. "I'll take a quick shower. Don't wait for me."

She rinsed and dried quickly and threw on a pair of shorts

and a tank top. In less than five minutes she had brushed her hair into a ponytail and returned to the cozy kitchen. Maybe she could have that talk with her father this morning.

"I hope you saved me some hotcakes. I could eat a whole plate."

Her father set down his cup of coffee and reached for the platter. "I'm not surprised, *mija*. You've been working very hard."

Debra smiled at him as he handed her the plate of bacon. "Racing is a tough business."

"I have new respect for you." *Papá* shook his fork first at Debra, then at Sterling. "You too." He took another bite and, after swallowing, continued. "I see how you get up early every morning and don't stop except to eat. I see how you sweat and strain. In all my life I never work *that* hard." His laughter punctuated his words, but his eyes were sincere.

"Then you understand how important it is to us?"

Her father put his fork down with a *clank.* "I can see how hard you work, *mija,* but I don't understand what you get out of the sport."

She glanced over at Sterling for support, but his gaze was on his plate. "What do famous athletes get out of any sport? They want to show the world they are the best. They want to prove they can overcome the odds." She picked at her pancake with her fork. "And there's always the prize money."

Papá shrugged. "So you want to be famous and win prizes. Then what? What happens when you can't ride no more?"

Heat coursed through Debra that had nothing to do with the sip of hot coffee she had just swallowed. Tears welled and spilled, unbidden, down her cheeks.

Her father folded his napkin on the table and stood. "Speaking of work, it's time I was off to do my own." He kissed *Mamá*'s cheek, placed his worn hat on his head, and hurried out the door.

A sob shook Debra's body. She covered her face with her napkin.

Her mother crossed the kitchen and stood behind Debra, wrapping her ample arms around her shoulders. "He is proud of you, my daughter."

"I want to believe that. More than anything."

Sterling leaned close. "Believe, *querida*."

Chapter Fourteen

Debra sprawled on the carpet in the garage, one leg straight up, stretching sore muscles. The door creaked open, letting in a shaft of sunlight and a rush of fresh air. She lowered her leg and sat upright to face her father.

"Sterling told me to make sure you don't work too hard."

Debra smiled at the thought of the Silverwing. He'd gone to San Diego for a couple of days to take care of some business. "I'm cooling down now."

"You miss him, don't you?" Her father sat on the edge of the bench, one leg bracing him and the other dangling over a corner. He held an apple in one hand but pressed on his chest with the other.

"Have to admit, I'm getting spoiled." Much more than spoiled, but she didn't dare admit to that.

"He seems like a good coach." *Papá* coughed, the harsh sound echoing in the silent garage.

Debra lifted her other leg and began to twist her ankle to stretch out the muscles. "I wouldn't be back in shape if Sterling hadn't been here."

He coughed again, the sound bouncing against the walls, against her heart.

Debra stilled, her leg still poised in midair. "Are you okay?"

Papá waved his hand. "It's nothing, *mija,* just a cough and some heartburn. Loving someone is more important than racing, I think."

She rotated her ankle again in earnest. "Loving Sterling

wouldn't be fair to him. If I get on a national team, we won't be able to see each other during the season."

Denying her feelings for Sterling grew more difficult each day. Not seeing him disturbed her also, but she didn't mention that either.

Papá tossed the apple in his hand and smiled. "When love is strong, there are ways to overcome distance. When I was in Mexico that time your *nana* was sick, I was away from *Mamacita* for months at a time."

Debra closed her eyes, remembering the tears her mother had shed during that awful period when her grandmother was so ill.

Debra crawled across the carpet to sit next to her father. "She missed you. We all did. That is why I can't let myself get too close to Sterling. I would miss him so much, like *Mamá* missed you."

"And that's a bad thing, *mija?*"

She pulled her legs up and tucked her chin on her knees. "It plays havoc with your concentration. I'd be thinking of Sterling instead of the race."

Papá handed her the apple, his loud guffaw echoing in the room. "I think it's too late. You no practice now like you did when he was here. I see you daydreaming about your handsome young man."

Debra groaned before she took a bite out of the apple, its tangy crunch soothing her dry throat. "You're right. What am I going to do?"

"Simple, *mija*. Love him."

"But I wanted to prove to you I could accomplish something."

He placed a lean hand on her head, as he had when she was a child. "I see how hard you work, if that's what you mean." His work-roughened fingers trailed down her cheek, and he nudged her chin up so that he could look her in the eye.

A sob caught in Debra's throat. "I want you to be proud of me. I never could do well in school. I tried, *Papá,* but—"

He took her partially eaten apple and set it on the bench, then grabbed her hands and pulled her up to sit beside him.

"Maybe you could try again."

Debra stared in front of her. The exercise equipment stood like mechanical ghosts in the still room. Sunlight filtered through the cracks in the walls and reflected off the dust motes in the air. A heavy weight pressed on her heart. He still didn't understand. She jumped up and paced across the room.

"Do you know how hard I tried to get good grades to please you?" She ran back and planted her feet squarely in front of him. "Do you have any idea of the torture I've put myself through, trying to win your approval?"

Tears coursed down her cheeks. She wiped at the tears and grabbed his hands, his skin feeling oddly cold and clammy.

Suddenly his body stiffened. He gasped and clutched at his chest. He crumpled out of Debra's grasp onto the floor. Terrified, she dropped to her knees beside him.

¡Papá!

Sterling pulled into Debra's parents' yard and parked his car in front of the garage. Something was wrong. Midweek and cars parked everywhere. He recognized some of the vehicles— Debra's brothers and sisters from the Bay area.

Still. No laughter. No music. None of the sounds that usually abounded when her siblings arrived home.

Sterling peeled off his sunglasses, tossed them onto the dash, and slid out of his car. He shoved the garage door open. Empty. He looked at his watch. Two o'clock. Debra should have been working out. He checked the rack and saw that her bike was still there.

Sterling slammed the garage door shut and jogged toward the house. He stepped up onto the back porch, noticing clothes pulled out of the washing machine but not hung out to dry. He tried the doorknob. The door creaked as he opened it.

"Debra?"

Silence.

The kitchen looked like a disaster area. Dirty plates littered the counter and tabletop. Food sat in pans on the stove and in the sink, spoiling in the heat.

Fear gripped Sterling's gut. He dashed through the living room and down the hall to Debra's room and saw traveling bags strewn about the floor.

The bed was made, her clothes put away. No sign of Debra. Or anyone, for that matter.

Sterling ran outside and into the garage. Frantic, he searched the room and saw what he hadn't noticed the first time. Round pieces of plastic that backed vital-signs monitors. A syringe wrapper. Other odd shapes of plastic strips.

Paramedics had been here.

His heart pounded.

Sterling darted to each piece of equipment, searching for signs of an accident. Her towel. He grabbed the soft cloth. Her scent drifted toward his nostrils. He squeezed the material in a grip of steel. Blood. Blood smeared on the folds of the towel.

Sterling raced out of the garage and jumped into his car. His fingers fumbled until he finally got the keys into the ignition. As he backed out of the driveway, he searched the passenger seat for his cell phone.

He dialed 911.

"Is this an emergency?"

Yes! he wanted to scream.

"Not exactly." He tapped the steering wheel while he explained. "You made an ambulance call to Vineyard Drive. I need to know where you took the patient."

Seconds ticked by like hours while the operator checked the records.

"The Valenzuelas'?"

"Yes." Relief and anxiety tore through him.

"County Hospital. It's east of town."

Sterling memorized the directions the woman gave and prayed there would be no traffic in his way.

What could have happened? Had she fallen?

Sterling barely noticed his surroundings as he maneuvered through the small town. Thankfully the traffic was light. At the hospital, he recognized Mr. Valenzuela's pickup. And was that Carlos' van? He slipped into the parking space next to the truck and jumped out of the car, his heart pumping much too fast.

He ran up the ramp, practically knocking down a man exiting as he swung open the door.

"Hey, partner. Take it easy."

"Sorry. Emergency room—which way?"

The man's scowl disappeared as he pointed down the hall to the left.

Sterling nodded and tore down the hall. Antiseptic odors, green walls. Open doorways stole the privacy of the sick. Sterling forced down bile threatening to rise up his throat.

He rounded a bend and came upon a nurses' station. Impatient and desperate, he slapped a hand onto the counter to get the attention of a nurse who was busy on the computer.

"Debra Valenzuela. Where is she?"

The nurse scrunched her brow, thinking. "Don't believe there's anyone here named Debra."

"Valenzuela?" he repeated.

Her face smoothed with recognition. She pointed down the hall. "Room 116."

Sterling neared the room with a mixture of dread and eagerness to see her. A loud wail echoed out of the vicinity of her room. A cacophony of voices. All in Spanish. Sterling recognized *Mamá*. And—

"Sterling."

A blur came at him, dark hair flying, and tumbled into his arms.

"Debra!"

Relief flooded through him in spite of the sobs wracking her body. He held on to her tightly. "What's going on?" he asked, mystified.

It took a moment for her to focus on his words. "It's *Papá*." She gulped. "He had a heart attack."

"Is he going to be all right?"

She shuddered and burrowed her head into the crook of his neck. Her arms tightened around him. He held her close.

"He's critical," she sobbed.

Sterling rocked her back and forth, letting her cry out her sorrow.

Debra couldn't believe that Sterling was there. She had just been hoping that he would come. A sob caught in her throat.

Sterling pulled her closer into his embrace. "I thought something had happened to *you*." His voice rumbled against her ear.

She glanced at his bowed head and saw the lines of stress creasing his brow. "I'm so glad you came."

"I'm here for you and your family. Whatever you need."

She knew he had been worried about her. She breathed in deeply.

A light began flashing above the door of her father's room. Nurses and doctors charged past them and rushed Debra's family out of the room.

Fear tore at Debra's insides as she stepped away from Sterling and grasped her mother's hands. "What happened?"

"He's had another attack."

Carlos held his mother tightly while she wailed hysterically. "It's not a major one," he reassured all of them. "He could have several more attacks in these first twenty-four hours."

"Will he live?" Debra asked, as she clutched at Sterling's arms.

"He is being treated and monitored by the doctors. We can only pray." Her brother reached for her and pulled her and Sterling close around *Mamá*.

Debra stood there as long as she could. Guilt tore at her. She jerked away from the group. "It's all my fault."

Startled eyes stared at her.

"In the garage. *Papá* and I. We got into an argument."

Sterling reached for her. "You can't blame yourself for this."

Debra backed away, even though she longed to throw herself into the comfort of his embrace. "No, I—"

A doctor stepped out of the room and came toward them.

Debra clutched Sterling's arm, her nails digging into his skin.

"How is he?" Carlos asked.

The doctor rubbed the back of his neck. "Stabilized for now. We'll keep a close eye on him." He glanced around at Debra and her family. "You folks should go on home and rest. We've sedated him and he'll be out for the night."

Mamá started to protest, but Carlos tightened his hold on her.

The doctor nodded. "We'll call if there are any complications."

Carlos stepped forward. "We'll stay for a while."

Relief flooded through Debra. She couldn't bear to leave, and she could tell that *Mamá* didn't want to either.

Carlos guided them into the waiting room. Sterling helped her mother onto one of the vinyl chairs. Debra sank into another and watched him in a fog, thankful for his take-charge attitude and again relieved that he was there.

Finally she let out a long breath, releasing some of the pent-up tension and emotion. She settled against the cold plastic and closed her eyes.

Dust clouded the yard days later as Debra watched her brothers and sisters drive away one by one with their families. Sterling came up beside her.

"Your father's comfortable in bed. Your mother's asleep. All the activity of bringing him home wore her out."

Debra wiped at a tear that had slipped out and made a track down her cheek. "She's still in shock. She needs the rest." She nodded toward the cars. "I'm glad they were able to be here to visit with *Papá* when we brought him home. He's doing so much better now."

"That's a blessing, Debra."

Debra took a deep breath, her body shuddering slightly from stress and emotion.

"It meant a lot to me to be with your family at this time."

Debra nodded, and sat in the double swing on the porch and patted the seat, inviting Sterling to sit next to her. The swing swayed back with his weight. She tucked her feet up and let the to-and-fro movement soothe her frazzled nerves.

"We were in the garage talking when he—" Her voice caught. She braced herself as he pushed his foot on the floor to keep the swing in gentle motion.

"It's okay, you don't have to talk about it."

She sat for several moments appreciating the fact that Sterling could wait patiently without pressing her. She gazed at the serene expression on his face and saw tenderness and love. "No, I want to. I need to."

She explained about the conversation with her father, watching Sterling as she spoke, wondering if this information would change his feelings for her. She hoped not, because she realized she truly did love him.

Love.

Such a small word that held a mountain of meaning.

"I know the heart attack was my fault."

Sterling stopped the swing and tugged her around to face him. "Didn't you say he often complained of heartburn?"

Debra nodded.

"Then it wouldn't have been your fault. Heartburn and coughing are signs of a heart attack." Sterling patted her hand. "It's a blessing he was with you, even if you were disagreeing. What would have happened if he'd had the attack somewhere alone?"

Debra stilled as his words registered. "He would have died if the paramedics hadn't come right away."

"Exactly. You saved his life by calling the ambulance. You were here for him, Debra."

She moved to look into his silver-gray eyes. "If I hadn't dislocated my shoulder, *Mamá* would have been all alone."

Relief flooded her. Determination surfaced also. With her father's health so precarious, now more than ever she had to prove her worth. But did she really want to be away from Sterling or her family in order to continue racing?

The screen door opened. Her mother stepped onto the porch and stood before Debra and Sterling. She held a worn leather-encased book in her hands. "I, too, am thankful that you were here to help me."

Debra straightened out of the swing. "Did you get enough rest?" she asked in Spanish.

Mamá shook her head, her dark hair pulling loose from the chignon at the nape of her neck. "I couldn't sleep." She held out the worn book. "I want you to see this."

Debra grasped the book and reverently fingered the yellowed pages. "It's a journal."

"*Papá*'s. I want you to read it."

Trembling, Debra held the book out to her mother. "No, I couldn't. It's his private—"

Her mother gently pushed Debra's hand and the book back to her.

Debra started to protest, but her mother shushed her and pointed to the red, green, and white ribbon trailing out of the book. "Do you remember giving your father that?"

Debra fingered the twelve-inch satin strip and shook her head.

"When you were six, you gave it to him for *Cinco de Mayo*."

Memories of a school picnic and parade celebrating the Mexican holiday flashed through her mind. "We all wore ribbons with Mexico's colors."

"And your class stood on the stage and sang '*De Colores*.'"

Sterling started to hum the popular Mexican folk song. *Mamá* made a faint attempt to smile, her dark eyes sad and wistful.

"*Papá* burst with pride that day. He came home and put that ribbon in his journal. And look, *mija*. Look at the page where the ribbon is."

Debra slid the book open and glanced at the old words.

Tucked in between the pages was one of her old report cards, and next to the poor grades he'd written in his wobbly scrawl, *May my Debra someday succeed.* Stricken, she gripped the book and stared at her mother.

Tears streamed down the older woman's weathered cheeks, and she quickly wiped at them with a corner of her apron. "He prayed that every day. For you, *mija.*"

Debra shuddered as one sob after another slipped past her guard. Her hair tumbled forward as she bent to kiss the book and ribbon. The smell of old leather, mixed with the scent of her father, filled her nostrils. She clutched the book close to her chest. She'd never done well in school.

Her mother brushed at the tears that slid down her cheeks. "He wants so badly for you to succeed. You are going to continue racing, aren't you?"

She felt Sterling stiffen behind her. "I don't know. Don't you need me here with you?"

"I can take care of your father. I want you to follow your dream."

"What does *Papá* want?"

"He doesn't understand about the racing yet. But he will."

"I tried to explain."

"He—we're traditional. It is difficult at our age to understand new ideas." She sat in a nearby patio chair, her shoulders slumped and weary. "But we see you work hard. Sterling helped too. He explained to *Papá* about the racing—that it is work and not just play."

Debra tucked the book in her lap and reached for Sterling's hand. His fingers wrapped around hers, and he squeezed them tightly. She owed this man so much. He loved her. She should tell him that she returned his love.

But how could she, when she needed to race again? For *Papá*.

Debra wiped at the sweat pouring down her brow. She slid off the turbo trainer, glared at Sterling, and tossed the damp towel onto the bench. "This is ridiculous."

Sterling's laughter echoed from where he was sitting near her father's workbench. "No pain, no gain."

"Easy for you to say. I'm sweating away ten pounds, and you're sitting there like you're at a resort."

Sterling stood up and grabbed another towel. " 'Sweating'? More like raising a slight glow."

Debra placed her hands on her hips and spread her feet wide apart. "You've been pushing me too hard."

He walked in front of her and handed her the towel. "Only because you've been slacking off lately."

Debra froze, partly from defiance, partly from knowing he spoke the truth. She grabbed the towel and wiped at her neck. "I've been worried about my father."

"He's doing fine." Sterling remained inches from her.

Debra backed up a step to give herself space. "I know, but for how long? What if he has another heart attack?"

Sterling spread out his hands. "We can't control that, but he's on the right medications for his condition. I'm game for a workout. Let's go for a bike ride."

Debra's interest was piqued. "Out on the old mill road?"

Sterling nodded.

"In the hills?"

"Beats moping around here."

Debra grabbed her bicycle and braced it against the wall while Sterling reached for his Silverwing cycle. "You're sure I'm ready for this?"

"You have good movement in your shoulder. The break from exercise while your father was in the hospital did it good." Sterling pushed his bike next to hers.

Debra reached across the bike and grabbed his water bottle. "I'll go fill these."

It took only a few minutes to fill the containers and tell her mother where they were headed. She looked at *Mamá* and knew her mother had been right. The older woman handled the job of taking care of her father perfectly, and the activity was better for her than sitting around.

Debra set the bottles on the counter and flexed her muscles. Primed and in peak condition. Sterling had been right about her situation too.

The pull of racing, the deep longing, tugged at her with more intensity each day. Now that her father was feeling better, she was eager to get back into the circuit.

Debra grabbed the bottles and started to head out the door when the phone rang.

"Can you get that, *mija*?" *Mamá* reached for the plastic containers of pills the doctor had prescribed for her father. "*Papá* needs his medicine."

Debra set down the water bottles and picked up the phone.

"Debra, is that you? This is Cindy."

Excitement coursed through Debra, as well as a measure of nostalgia. "It's great to hear from you. I'm just starting to ride again."

"When are you going to join us?"

"Sterling says I should be ready in a couple of weeks."

"How's it working out with him?" From Cindy's tone she could tell the question held a double meaning.

Debra decided to ignore the personal relationship and stick to the cycling. "He's been wonderful at coaching me back into shape. My family thinks he's Mr. Perfect."

"And do you?"

Yes!

"We're getting along." That was an understatement. She smiled. "What races have you guys done?"

"We haven't gone to many more out-of-state events. Without you, our star cyclist, it isn't economically practical." Mingled with the background ringing of the cash register, a sigh sounded across the line. "Marilyn and the others are coming along under Ralph's tutelage, but they're not up to par with the pros yet."

Debra twisted the cord around her finger. "And Mary-Reva—have you heard any word about her?"

"She's been winning. The other riders from the Orange-Lite team placed high also."

Her stomach tightened with envy. She should have been the one placing first. "I can beat Mary-Reva."

"Get yourself into shape. You could have a good chance to win the Ore-Ida Challenge."

"I'll be there." Debra gripped the phone. After the conversation ended, she hung up, grabbed the water bottles, rushed out the door, and told Sterling the news.

"Ralph and Cindy want me back on the team. I told them a couple of weeks."

"I don't see why not."

"I'm ready to go today." Debra handed Sterling the water bottles.

"I'm glad to see your enthusiasm to ride has picked up again." Sterling placed the bottles in the cages on each of the bikes.

Debra grabbed her bike and straddled it, ready to begin. "*Mamá* seems to be doing fine without my help." She started pedaling out of the yard.

Sterling rode up beside her. "What about your father? Are you riding for the thrill of racing or to prove something to him?"

Debra slackened her pace. "I still want to make him proud of me. Besides, that longing I told you about, it seems to be more intense."

"Winning races isn't going to satisfy those yearnings."

Her feelings told her she longed to win—she'd done that. She longed for *Papá*'s love—she was beginning to earn that. Debra watched Sterling cycle beside her. She longed for his love—she could have that.

Could Sterling be right?

Debra lowered her head and pumped harder. "I have to find out for myself."

Chapter Fifteen

For the next two weeks, Sterling rode with Debra daily. With each outing, Debra could feel her strength growing and the longing intensifying. It was after such a ride, while eating lunch with her parents, that Sterling hit her with the news.

"The Ore-Ida Challenge is a month away. It's time to get you back in the races." He piled beans onto his tortilla and took a bite.

Debra dropped her fork and clenched her fists to keep from jumping up and shouting. Out of the corner of her eye she could see that her parents sat still, awaiting her response.

"You're serious?" She glanced at her parents, missing them already, and then gazed at Sterling. She would miss the proximity to Sterling she'd enjoyed while he lived in her parents' house.

Sterling ate his tortilla as if he were discussing the local weather. No emotion crossed his features. "Talked to Ralph this morning. He's got the Desert Roadrunners racing in Prescott for the Skull Valley race next weekend and then the Twilight series in Tucson."

"It'll be cooler in Prescott. It's a good place to start back in." Debra forgot about her lunch as plans dashed through her head.

"You going to stay with her?" Her father's question hung in the air.

Debra locked gazes with Sterling. Her heart thudded. She needed to focus all of her attention on the racing, but thoughts of him leaving tore at her soul.

146

Sterling set down his glass and returned Debra's stare. "I'm heading back to San Diego."

"You aren't returning to the Silverwings?"

Papá reached for Debra's hand, his grip surprisingly strong. "You need to race. Sterling needs to go." He peered at Sterling and gave him a look of warning.

Unperturbed, Sterling nodded. "Don't worry about a thing. Debra will have the opportunity to follow her dream." He helped himself to another tortilla and looked at Debra. "I won't let emotional entanglements get in the way of your goal. When we get together, it'll be with a lifelong commitment."

She glared at her father and then at Sterling. "Sounds like you two have everything all planned out." She grabbed a tortilla and shoved a spoonful of beans onto it. "Did you think to consult me?"

Sterling frowned. "I thought that's what you wanted."

Debra slammed her tortilla onto her plate and stood. The abrupt motion knocked the chair over backward, but she paid no attention to it. Leaving it lying on the floor, she flew out of the kitchen.

A cacophony of Spanish trailed through the window, which she ignored. "I love Sterling," she murmured as she tore across the grass. "I want him to be with me, but will I be able to race?"

She could tell it was Sterling waiting for her to turn around.

"I thought you would be thrilled about the news."

"It won't work, you know." She shrugged, the action tossing her hair into the breeze.

He moved beside her, the scent of her peach shampoo mingling with the smells of the flowers and grass. "You don't expect to win?"

She crossed her arms in front of her chest and turned to face him. "I'm ready to race again. But that's not what I'm talking about. You know that."

Sterling's heart skipped a beat. She looked so fragile standing there, the sun reflecting in her eyes, eyes that were clouded with mixed emotions. He longed to pull her into his arms and smooth away the frown.

"You know how I feel about you," he said.

"That's why it won't work. I still need to win. But I won't be able to stop thinking about you."

"We have two days to get back to Arizona." He placed his hands on his hips to keep from reaching out for her. "I'll arrange for a truck to come by and pick up the equipment."

"Sterling, I—"

Sterling raised a hand to stop her. "Call Ralph. He'll see that you're set to race."

"I'm afraid."

Sterling stared in amazement. "To race?"

"Yes. No." She paced to the garage and back. "I know I can do it. But I'm not sure about us. I mean—I want us to be together, but I'm not sure . . ."

Sterling waited until she returned to him. "Don't think about it now. Let's ride into the foothills. We can head for the granite outcropping that overlooks the valley."

Relief softened her expression, making his heart ache for her. "That sounds like a plan. I'll go tell *Mamá* we'll be gone for the rest of the day. You get the bikes ready." She headed toward the house. "I'll be back in fifteen minutes."

It took almost two hours for them to cycle through the foothills and reach the granite rocks protruding from the Sierra mountain range. Sterling dismounted, leaned his bike under a tree, and stretched his muscles. Debra placed her bike next to his and climbed onto the large flat rock. Sterling followed and stood beside her, staring across the San Joaquin Valley that extended for miles below.

"I'm hardly out of breath. I can't believe it was only a month ago that I was puffing like a steam engine." Debra brushed back her hair and smiled at him.

"It's a miracle." He mimicked the television advertisement.

She reached out and playfully slugged him. Sterling moaned with mock pain as he grabbed his arm. He saw the look in her eye and stopped.

"This is right, isn't it? This love between us," she said softly.

Sterling tensed. *Love.* Was she saying . . .

"Maybe I should just quit racing."

His breath caught in his throat. "What are you talking about?" His arms felt numb as he dropped them to his sides.

She shrugged and stepped away from him. Her gaze encompassed the view, but he doubted she really saw it. "When we're together like this, the racing doesn't seem so important."

Wasn't that what he'd wanted? He longed for her total commitment, but he knew it would never work. "You would resent me later, when you realized you'd passed up your dreams—for me."

A frown creased her brow. "That's what I'm afraid of." She walked to the edge of the rock. "I'm confused. I used to know exactly what I wanted."

Grabbing her hand and guiding her to a safer position on the rock, he sat and pulled her down beside him. "I think your father's heart attack scrambled your emotions, but you still have the same goals, the same desires. It would be best to follow through with them."

What am I saying? A shudder tore through him. He bent his legs, leaned one elbow on his knee, and pressed at his temples as if he could erase the visions passing through his mind—visions of loneliness while Debra raced abroad.

"How are we going to do that?"

Sterling knew, but pain coursed through him at having to say it. "I'll return to the Silverwings. You go back to your team and win those races."

Her gasp of despair didn't help his resolve. "We can't just ignore our feelings of . . ."

He put a finger to her lips. "Don't say it. Leaving you is going to be difficult enough without complicating our relationship further."

"I thought that was what you wanted."

He did. How he longed to whisk her away and start a life together. But he could see now more than ever that he had to let her play out her desire to succeed. Taking her from that would leave a seed of discontent to grow until it strangled their love.

"You've recovered from your injuries. There's nothing to stop you." *Except me.* He'd raced enough to know that he could hamper her concentration—concentration she would need to stay on top of the fierce competition. Until she did that, she could never resolve her issues with her father.

Sterling breathed in deeply, memorizing the scent of her. It would be a long wait.

Debra stood on the lawn of her parents' house and watched Sterling drive away. She longed to run after him. She should insist he stay. She wanted to hold him and never let go. She stood still, rooted to the spot.

"It's for the best," she whispered into the breeze. "You need to be back with your team."

Tears slid down her cheeks. Tears that she ignored. Taking a deep breath, she spun on her heel and headed for the garage. With shaky fingers she grabbed her bike and wheeled it outside. Pausing, she glanced back at the house, and then, with a shake of her head, she climbed onto the bike.

Wind whipped past her tear-streaked face as she pedaled onto the road. Her heart felt as if it had been ripped to shreds. Longings threatened to choke her. Sterling would be gone when she returned. She didn't dare look back.

Debra placed the CLOSED sign on the door of Desert Cyclery and turned to Ralph. "What's next on the agenda?"

Ralph straightened the counter of the shop before turning off the cash register. "It's time to get you to another big race. You've done a miraculous job placing first in the last two Arizona meets."

"I didn't really have any tough competition." Debra tried to build up enthusiasm for her success. The victories felt hollow now. Not only did she have her father's respect to worry about, but Sterling was not there to share in the celebrations. And longings still tugged at her.

Cindy pulled the shades down in the large front window. "I was thinking the same thing. How about the Nevada City Classic? The elevation changes and mountain cycling will be good preparation for the Ore-Ida Challenge."

"You can handle it?" Debra asked, knowing that Ralph and Cindy didn't have tremendous financial resources. The Nevada City Classic would cost quite a bit to transport them and their equipment to the California Sierras.

"Since we stopped going to the out-of-state races, we were able to save." He smiled at Debra as she locked the display cases. "And since our star began shining last spring, our business has picked up, not to mention the new sponsors the team has acquired."

"I've still got some of my last winnings," Debra offered, as she handed Ralph the key and then folded T-shirts customers had left on the table.

"Hang on to it. We may need it when we get there."

Cindy nudged Ralph and turned to Debra. "Can you believe we're going to the Ore-Ida Challenge?"

"I can't believe we're discussing the Nevada City Classic, let alone the Ore-Ida Challenge," Debra exclaimed as she stacked the folded shirts. "After the accident, I was beginning to wonder if I'd be riding at all."

"Riding with the pros has always been your goal," Cindy teased.

"But it seemed so far away. Being so close now seems like a dream."

"You'd better wake up. This dream is going to be coming true real soon."

The Nevada City Classic proved to be beneficial toward building Debra up for the high altitude. After going months without racing in events with trade teams, she was able to hold her own and placed first.

The Orange-Lites had not entered the Nevada City Classic. Instead they had stayed back east. But several small racing squads were competing in the California Sierras, which gave the Desert Roadrunners an opportunity to work on their team strategy.

After the Nevada City Classic, Ralph and Cindy managed to get the team into a couple more national prestige events. By the time they were settled into their accommodations in Boise, Idaho, for the Ore-Ida Challenge, Debra was physically ready for the twelve-day series of grueling races.

Emotional readiness was another matter. A month had passed since she'd seen Sterling, and the yearning for him had only intensified. This week she hadn't been able to contact her parents. Her brothers and sisters had been evasive and unconcerned about their parents' whereabouts. Perhaps her father was not doing so well and they didn't want to worry her before the big event.

To top those concerns were the deep longings that clawed at her sense of calm. The closer she came to accomplishing her goal, the more doubtful she became that achieving victory in a race would bring her peace.

On the morning of the first race, Ralph made sure Debra and the Desert Roadrunners were up in plenty of time to catch the transport provided to the starting point in the small town of Emmett, Idaho. The first stage, a seventy-eight-mile race from Emmett to Nampa, was a challenge for everyone. Debra barely placed in the top ten. After the high winds and heavy rain, the mood of the riders changed from excitement and anticipation to one of serious intent and determination to survive. A major crash at the finish line didn't help boost morale either. Nancy Thompson of the Orange-Lites was taken by ambulance to the hospital.

The following stages served to weed out more of the competition, especially the thirty-one-mile climb of stage three's

"Round the Horn" from Loman to Stanley. Several teams dropped out because of equipment failure, injuries, illness, and the weather. The Roadrunners, who were used to climbs but not the high altitudes, lost two of their team members. Debra, Marilyn, and the other two remaining hung in there, but barely.

"How's the shoulder?" Ralph asked, when she came in for a pit stop during the seventh day's race.

She curled her arm and grimaced. "My lungs and legs burn so badly, I barely notice pain elsewhere."

"That's when you're in danger. The pain is your body's warning to take it easy. If you ignore your shoulder, you could cause more problems."

Debra slumped, and she hung her head. "You sound like Sterling."

Ralph squirted her with water, sending chills across her skin. "I take that as a compliment."

Debra hoisted herself onto her bicycle. If only Sterling were here. Twice she thought she'd seen the Silverwing. Wishful thinking. Yet she *felt* as if Sterling were close. Perhaps because she had relied so heavily on his past advice and training these past days. His expertise was the edge that kept her in league with the elite.

She glanced over her shoulder, searching the crowds as she pedaled onto the road.

Sterling perused the crowded street of the small town in Idaho. Cyclists in bright colors moved within the space directly behind the starting line. Bicycles wove in and out among the crowd of sixty women racing in the challenge. Tourists and fans lined the perimeters of the narrow street. Local news crews struggled to make sense out of the pandemonium.

Debra wasn't anywhere in sight. He was glad, because he and Ralph had decided it was best for her not to see him until the challenge was over. They didn't want any distraction to cloud her concentration. Yet it brought such torturous joy to catch glimpses of her.

Sterling recognized many cyclists. Several walked by, surprised to see him there instead of with the Silverwings. He didn't bother to explain.

Hugh Ashford pushed by him, stopped and stared for a moment, and offered his hand. "Don't tell me you're a spectator these days. Here to see Valenzuela?"

Sterling shook hands but had no intention of discussing Debra with Ashford. "Heard the Orange-Lites placed third in the Nestlé Foods Classic. What happened? Thought you'd place first."

"There was one hotshot from back east. She was riding independent." Ashford stepped aside to let a group of spectators pass. "Probably a European riding under an alias. Goes by Julie."

Sterling glanced around at the crowd. "Is she racing here?"

"Yes." Ashford groaned. "So, you with Valenzuela?"

Sterling debated whether to tell the truth or let Ashford think he was with Debra. "She doesn't know I'm here."

Ashford studied him for several moments. His brow furrowed, and then he smiled. "Good. We're short a cyclist since we lost Nancy Thompson. I'm thinking of offering her a position on the team to help finish out the season. I wouldn't want anyone getting in the way."

Sterling's pulse hammered through his body and pounded in his head. "Does she know that?"

Ashford's laugh grated down his spine. "I'm waiting to see how she holds up." He slapped his thigh. "But she looks good."

She didn't look good. She looked terrific. Her dreams were about to be fulfilled. He should be ecstatic. So why did he feel as if his world had collapsed?

After he left Ashford, he walked around, avoiding more people he knew. Time dragged whenever he was away from Debra. These past weeks had been pure torture. What was he going to do if she accepted Ashford's offer?

Sterling searched the cyclists for a glimpse of her. He saw several brunets, but none of them was Debra. After a quick glance back at the Orange-Lite van and Ashford, he took a deep breath, determined to stick with his resolution to let Debra fulfill her dream.

He treasured Debra's love. If that meant letting her go to race with another team in the States and in Europe, then that's how it would have to be. He couldn't imagine holding her back. Not when he knew her dreams.

A flash of green caught his eye. *Debra.* She and Ralph were talking. Before he could react, Debra swung around and spotted him. How, he couldn't imagine. There must have been at least forty people milling about between them. Seeing her wave lifted his spirits. Seeing her maneuver her bicycle through the crowd toward him sent them soaring.

Excitement bubbled from her as she bounced on her toes. "What are you doing here?"

"Came to see a winner." How he wanted to hold her in his arms.

Evidently the thought crossed her mind as well. She started to reach for him. He took a step back. Her face sobered as she dropped her arms. "You haven't been with your team?"

He shrugged. "I had some business to take care of. Are you enjoying the event?"

She stared at him for several moments, her eyes boring into his, as if she didn't believe him. With a shake of her shoulders, she broke the intent look and gazed out across the crowd. "I've never been in an event this size. There's TV coverage and everything."

He clenched his fists behind him to keep from brushing her hair from her face. "Get used to the hype, *querida.* If you go to Europe, there'll be even more of this."

Her knuckles turned white where she gripped the handlebars, and she restlessly bounced the front of her bike up and down. "How wonderful. All of these people have worked hard to train and get into shape. There should be national recognition for their efforts."

"You sound like a typical cyclist now," he teased, wishing they could both say what they really wanted to.

I love you.

"Next you'll be telling me there should be the same money here as in Europe. You'll be comparing cycling to football and baseball."

Debra made a brave attempt to laugh. "You've been around too long, Sterling. You know too much." She gestured at their surroundings. "This is all new and exciting to me."

Unable to resist any longer, he tucked a strand of hair behind her ear. "That's just what I've been telling myself."

Debra grasped his hand and held it tightly. "I've missed you so much."

Her caring touched his heart. Several people he knew eyed them curiously. *Let them.*

Reluctantly she stepped away from him. "I have to go now. Where are you staying? Will I see you later?"

He didn't want to tell her that he had flown her parents to Idaho. He'd already broken his promise to Ralph about talking to her himself. She only had four more races to go. "After the challenge is over. I have a surprise for you."

Her eyes widened. "How can I race, knowing that?"

"Forget I'm here. I don't want to ruin your concentration." He grasped her hand. "Don't forget what you're here for. I'll be keeping positive thoughts for a win."

She frowned for a moment as if she would protest, and then she chuckled. "That's not fair. That doesn't give the others much chance."

Sterling sobered. "Each of you will ride to your fullest capacity."

"Then how are you so sure that I'll win?"

"Because you have done your part to prepare your body and your mind. Now you need to believe. When you do, you'll finish knowing that you did the best possible."

She stared at him for several long seconds. Sterling shifted, wondering if he'd gone too far. She smiled. "Thanks." She replaced her helmet and headed for the starting line.

Sterling watched her ride away, his heart pounding with regret, sorrow, and joy.

Chapter Sixteen

With the exception of the Orange-Lites and a few of the European women, the pack rode more sluggishly than usual. From the talk around, some of the women had partied too much. At a big event such as the Ore-Ida Challenge, sponsors wanted to fraternize with their cyclists.

At first Debra rejoiced that the others weren't up to par. Her running into Sterling had affected her more than she wanted to admit. Had he been there all week? Why hadn't he talked to her? It was pure chance that she'd seen him before the race. Would he be there at the finish line?

Debra pedaled hard, her breath catching as she tried to remain focused. Having the rest of the pack sluggish proved to be a disadvantage. Debra had no one to balance out the team power of the Orange-Lites. The European women would not make an effort to work together against the Orange-Lites; they wanted to stand out on their own. Consequently Debra placed third in the race.

"What happened out there?" Ralph grabbed the bike as Debra climbed off and handed it over.

Debra took in deep breaths. "Sterling. Have you seen him?"

Ralph lowered his head and avoided her eyes. "Sterling?"

She took off her helmet and shook her hair loose. "I saw him before the race."

"You sure it wasn't someone who looked like him?" Ralph took her helmet and hung it up in the van.

"We talked. Said he had a surprise for me." Before Ralph

could answer, she started walking away from the van, periodically standing on tiptoe to see over the crowd.

Blond heads appeared everywhere, but not Sterling's. Where was he? Debra returned to the van. "Did you know he was in town? Where would he be staying? Why isn't he here with us?"

Ralph shrugged. Debra paced behind the van while he loaded her gear. When he had finished, he grasped her by the elbow and guided her into the passenger seat of the vehicle. "We have events to go to this afternoon, and Cindy is waiting at the hotel. Let's go."

Debra climbed into the van, stretching her neck to see through the crowd as Ralph drove to their lodgings. Once they left the staging grounds, she leaned her head back against the seat and sighed. Had she imagined Sterling? Somehow she'd find him again. She hadn't been participating in the social events sponsored by the college town in honor of the cyclists.

Today she would.

Later that afternoon, Debra attended the fish fry put on by the Clear Springs Trout Company in conjunction with the town of Buhl. As sponsors of the day's race, they had built quite a reputation for the feast. Debra walked around the grounds. Normally she would enjoy attending this outdoor event, since it was held early enough for her to get her rest.

Not today.

Sterling was not there.

Debra straightened her denim skirt for the tenth time and glanced around for the Silverwing. Several townspeople stopped to chat. She tried to be social, but she couldn't focus on their words. After eating what she could of the fish dinner, she looked around for Cindy and Ralph, hoping to talk them and the rest of the team into going back to the hotel.

Crowds of people milled about the park. Flags and banners splashed color against the clear blue sky. Smells of frying fish and barbecue wafted in the slight breeze. Debra sidestepped several groups of cyclists as she worked her away toward the parking lot.

"Debra." Someone calling her name caught her attention, and she turned.

Mary-Reva waved from across the courtyard and came toward her. Debra debated about pretending she hadn't heard or seen her but finally forced a smile and met her halfway.

"Great race today," Debra complimented her rival on her win.

"It's about time I beat you to the finish." Mary-Reva softened her words with a chuckle and a wink.

Debra shrugged, the action brushing back her hair that hung loose across her shoulders.

Mary-Reva sipped her juice and eyed Debra closely. "You're doing great out there, Debra. You're my main competition."

Debra smiled as she grabbed a bottle of Perrier from the tray of a passing waiter. "Julie is a major threat also." She referred to the French cyclist who was slated to contend in the Olympics.

"Which is what I want to talk to you about." Mary-Reva guided her away from the others. "We have team support most of the race. But by the time we reach the last leg, it usually ends up being the three of us."

Debra nodded as she followed Mary-Reva to the edge of the crowd. The precedent the three of them had set did not follow the typical pattern for women cyclists. Most of the time a team rode in a pack the whole distance. Rarely did the individuals break away on daring sprints as Debra and Julie had. That had forced Mary-Reva to do the same. The rest of the cyclists had remained behind in the pack.

"Hugh is watching you closely. I think he's contemplating offering you a place on our team."

Debra's attention perked up. "And what do you think about that?" She gripped the cold bottle as she studied Mary-Reva's face.

"You're good, and I like your ethics." Sincerity showed in her eyes. "I think you'd make a great addition to the Orange-Lites."

Debra almost choked on the icy water. Quickly she swallowed, hoping she didn't come off looking like a flustered kid. "That comment makes up for my third place today." She thanked Mary-Reva, wondering how much clout the cyclist had in selecting teammates, while at the same time she pushed away the images of Sterling that surfaced. How could her heart ache so much when her goal was finally within reach?

Mary-Reva stopped walking and turned to Debra. "So how about trying some teamwork?"

Surprised, Debra cleared her throat and set the rest of the Perrier on a nearby table. "What did you have in mind?"

Mary-Reva pulled Debra farther away from the crowd. "I propose we work together as a team. When we've dusted the rest and left them behind, we operate together to keep Julie in back of us. That way we can pull in the first and second place money."

Debra stared, wondering what Ralph and Cindy would have to say about this. What would Sterling advise? It sounded like a safe plan of action, especially as she wanted to ultimately ride with Mary-Reva as an Orange-Lite.

"And if it's just you and me?"

"We're on our own. For blood." Mary-Reva chuckled good-naturedly. "And of course it only applies when we've lost our team support."

"When both of us have lost our teams," Debra clarified.

A glint of mischief shone in Mary-Reva's eye. "But if I leave you in the dust right from the start, then you're on your own."

"In your dreams." Debra placed her hands on her hips. "You know that I'm always right up there with you."

Mary-Reva groaned. "Unfortunately, yes." Then her expression sobered. "Actually, Debra, you've been good for me. You've pushed me to surpass the rider I was."

Debra smiled. "Then let's show those European women what American cyclists can do."

Mary-Reva held out her hand, and Debra shook it.

A masculine cough sounded behind them. Debra turned, hoping to see Sterling coming up beside her.

Mary-Reva pulled her hand from Debra's and stepped aside. "What's up, Ralph?"

Debra's shoulders sagged with disappointment. Ralph and Cindy stood there, arm in arm.

He nodded toward Debra's still outstretched hand. "Looks ominous. What're you two cooking up?"

Debra lowered her arm. "Strategy."

Mary-Reva tilted her head toward Debra and explained what they had discussed. Debra watched Ralph closely, hoping he would approve.

"Sounds like good teamwork to me."

Mary-Reva nodded, pivoted away, and headed back to her team.

Debra let out her breath in a *whoosh*. "That was a surprise."

Ralph tugged Cindy closer to him. "Just watch yourself out there. She may offer teamwork, but she's out to win."

Cindy stroked his cheek and smiled. "My big protector."

Tears welled unexpectedly in Debra's eyes. Where was *her* knight in shining armor? *Her* Prince Charming?

The next two stages were the individual trials and criterium. Debra and Mary-Reva did not have an opportunity to try out their new pact. Mary-Reva placed first in the individual trials, and Debra placed first in stage ten's criterium.

It wasn't until the last twenty miles of stage eleven that Debra, Julie, and Mary-Reva lost the rest of the cyclists in a daring breakaway. Hammering to the finish, in spite of over a hundred exhausting miles behind them, Debra and Mary-Reva placed with seconds between them, leaving them going into the last-stage criterium in a tie for first place.

Debra's legs burned with excruciating pain as she cycled up

to the van where Cindy and Ralph huddled on the lee side of the vehicle, away from the chilling breeze. Out of breath, she started to greet them, when their private conversation carried words that chilled her to the bone. Heart pounding, she moved closer to hear more.

"I know her father wants to talk to her, but you saw what happened the day she saw Sterling." Determination rang in Ralph's voice. "It took her two days to come back to first place. Sterling has stayed out of the picture. They have to also."

"I hope you're right. We only have one day to go." Cindy sounded worried. "She can see them all tomorrow."

Debra shook her head. Her parents? Were they here in Idaho? And Sterling. Hiding from her?

Debra shoved her bike against the van, making enough noise to catch the attention of an army. "What's going on?" she demanded.

Cindy and Ralph broke apart, looking guilty. "Debra, you were fantastic." Cindy lifted her arms and cheered.

Before Debra could respond, Ralph had her in his arms and swung her around. "Congratulations. You're now tied for first." He set her down and turned to put her bike into the van's rack.

Cindy and Ralph both avoided Debra's eyes. They were suddenly very busy putting her gear away.

In spite of the fact that she had no sensation left in her legs and that her brain felt as it it were filled with putty, Debra generated a spark of outraged energy. "I want to see my parents."

Ralph took her elbow and propelled her toward the winner's stage. "A criterium. That's all that's left, and you're great in that event."

"They're here. I heard you talking. I want to see them." What could Cindy and Ralph have been thinking? Did they believe she was that weak that she couldn't deal with Sterling or her family? Debra shuddered at the realization that they could be right.

Cindy caught up with them and slipped her arm through

Debra's. "Let's get your prize. We'll talk about it after the ceremony—when we're alone and have privacy."

Debra glanced at her teammates and the crowds cheering her as she approached the stage. Noise assailed her senses. The wind carried the smells of popcorn and other food from the vendors. Debra stumbled. Ralph and Cindy tightened their hold.

"Get a grip. Just hang in there until this is over," Ralph murmured close to her ear.

The awareness that she was close to victory didn't sink in until after she received her bouquet of flowers and the prize money. The news media asked several questions, cameras flashed, and the crowd cheered as Debra tried to gather her strength, while at the same time trying to control the inner turmoil.

Papá.

Sterling.

Debra closed her eyes as blackness closed in. Vaguely she was aware of falling—falling into a deep hole.

Sterling stared at Debra as she accepted her prize money and flowers. Something was wrong. Her face had paled. Her fingers shook; he could tell even from this distance.

Not caring anymore if she saw him, he stepped from under a vendor's umbrella to get a better look. Debra wobbled. Hair blew in front of her face so he couldn't see her eyes.

"She's going to faint." Sterling shoved his way through the crowd.

Before he could get near, Debra collapsed on the stage. Officials surrounded her, and a siren sounded beyond the crowd. Fear clutched at Sterling's heart as the wail pierced his ears.

Sterling saw Ralph and Cindy trying to ascend the steps to the stage. He headed for them, worried he wouldn't have much better luck. Security was tight around the cyclists, especially the ones on the stage. "Let me through."

Sterling reached Ralph's side and grabbed his arm. "What's the matter?"

Ralph looked dazed for a moment before he recognized Sterling. He shook his head. "She was upset."

Cindy crowded in between the two men. "She heard us talking about you and her parents. She knows they're here and wants to see them. And you."

Sterling let out his breath. "I was afraid this might happen. We should have been up front and let her know."

Cindy wiped at the tears streaming down her face. "But she wants so badly to win. We couldn't risk the distraction."

Ralph pulled Cindy into his arms. "It's obvious we made the right decision. Look what's happened now that she knows."

Sterling struggled with impatience and annoyance. None of that mattered now. Debra needed him, and he couldn't get past the guards.

Movement onstage caught his attention, and he turned from Ralph to see Debra sitting up.

He waved his arms and shouted. "I'm over here!"

Debra peered past one of the officials. Her eyes brightened when she saw him. She pointed in his direction and spoke to the men and women hovering over her. The woman turned and motioned him onstage. Relief coursed through Sterling as he mounted the steps two at a time.

"Don't get up," he ordered when she started to rise. "Wait a minute until you're sure you have your equilibrium."

"I'm fine." Her quivering lips and flushed face belied her words.

Voices clamored, but Sterling could not focus on what the officials were saying. He looked around, impatient and wanting to get Debra away from all the attention. Bending, he took a deep breath and hoisted her into his arms.

One of the officials stepped in front of him. "You can't do that. Wait until the paramedics look at her."

Debra reached out and grabbed the official's hand. "I'm fine. Sterling's my trainer. He'll take care of me."

Her words warmed his heart. If only he could do that—for the rest of her life.

"I'll take her to the medics' truck." He nodded in the direction of the approaching paramedics. "She needs attention, but not here onstage."

The officials weren't happy, but before they could protest further, he descended the steps and headed toward the first-aid vehicle.

Minutes seemed like hours while Sterling paced outside the van. What should he do? Let her see her parents? He had wanted to avoid distracting her from the race, but it was too late. She would be more upset not seeing them now that she knew they were there. He took a deep breath.

So close. One race to go, and her dreams would come true. Sterling took out his handkerchief and wiped the sweat from his brow.

Silence chilled the cool evening air, as Debra sat staring out of the backseat window of the Desert Cyclery van as it rolled through the streets of Boise toward the hotel. Every light turned red. Traffic swarmed in front of them, blocking their route.

Ralph mumbled. Cindy faced front in the passenger seat. Sterling sat beside Debra, his jaw clenching and unclenching as the tension thickened. Marilyn and the others had taken Sterling's van and driven ahead of them to the hotel.

Impatient and restless, Debra turned to glare at Sterling. "Do you have such little faith in me that you didn't think I could handle seeing my parents?"

Sterling shifted until he faced her squarely. His silver-gray gaze bored unflinchingly into hers. "I know how important your father's opinion is to you." He gestured toward Ralph. "I—we couldn't take the risk that he would upset you."

And they thought not telling her wouldn't upset her even more? Debra tugged on the strings of the hood of the sweatshirt she'd tossed over her Lycra racing outfit after Cindy's massage. "How long have they been here?"

Cindy swiveled in her seat to look at Debra. "They arrived the first day of the race."

"And you knew they were here?"

Cindy nodded and lowered her head, unable to look Debra in the eye. Debra shook her head in disbelief.

Ralph pulled up in front of the hotel, and Debra waited for Sterling to let her out.

He held out his hand to help her down. "I'm coming up with you."

Debra paused, wondering if she would need the moral support, and decided she did. "Might as well, since you were all in this together."

Debra brushed past him and hurried into the foyer of the plush hotel. Her parents would not have been able to afford this place for a day, let alone a week. She saw the elevators and waited there for Sterling. "Are you paying for this?"

"Does it matter?"

Debra stepped into the elevator, fighting a mixture of emotions that ranged from hurt pride to loving adoration that Sterling would do such a thing for her family.

Sterling followed her, and as soon as the door *whooshed* shut, he turned to her. "I'm sorry you had to find out this way. We wanted it to be a surprise."

Tears welled, and she swallowed hard, forcing them down. She breathed in his woodsy scent. This was exactly where she wanted to be and had longed to be for the past month.

"I missed you," she murmured. "I was frantic to find you after I saw you the other day."

"These past few days have been pure torture." He lifted her chin with one finger and brushed his lips against hers.

Tendrils of pleasure and joy raced through Debra, revitalizing exhausted muscles and her aching heart. Too soon the elevator stopped and the doors opened. Sterling grasped her shoulders and gently pushed her into the hall and to a door several feet away. "Your parents are waiting. I called them from the staging grounds."

Like a splash of cold water, the mention of her parents

sobered Debra. She straightened her sweatshirt, wishing she'd taken the time to stop at her hotel to shower and change.

Before she could think of how to react, *Mamá* threw open the door. "*Mija,* you've arrived." Her voice filled the hallway with its warmth and lilting Spanish, chasing away any doubts or concerns.

She hugged her mother, drinking in the wildflower scent of her hair and skin, a fragrance that brought floods of memories. "I'm so glad you're here. Have you seen any of the races?"

Her father crowded in from behind and wrapped his arms around both women. "We saw you win. Several times. We're so proud of you."

Debra glanced over her shoulder at Sterling, who rocked on his heels with hands in his pockets and a smile on his face. "Thank you." She mouthed the words.

He nodded and mouthed the words, "I love you."

In a flurry of activity and talking, Debra was whisked inside. It didn't matter that there was a fantastic view out the windows or plush furniture inside. The warmth and laughter of old family jokes brought a sense of home to this city in Idaho.

"Isn't it *fantástico?*" *Papá* waved his hands. "Sterling finds us this great place to stay. He is like a son."

Her mother motioned for Debra to follow her. "This is our room. It's so big. And Sterling stays there." She pointed to a door across the suite and then stepped into a third room. "There is room for you too. Can you stay tonight?"

"I don't have any of my things." Debra eyed the luxurious accommodations, heard the deep voices of Sterling and her father in the background, and wished with all her heart she could stay.

Mamá threw up her hands and hurried to Sterling. "She says she can't stay. You must do something."

Debra hurried to explain. "My things—"

Sterling rose from the couch and headed for the door. "I'll catch a cab to your hotel and grab your stuff."

Debra started to protest, when Sterling lifted up a hand. "Don't say a word. Besides, I need to pick up the van for the morning. I'll get your things while I'm there."

His words brought her up short. "I didn't even think—"

"You've been focused on the race, which is as it should be." He stuck his arms into his jacket and shrugged it onto his shoulders. "Catch up on all the news, and then get into the tub. You'll be going to bed when I return. You have a big day tomorrow."

Debra chuckled and saluted with two fingers to her forehead. "We're certainly back to the good ol' days. Aren't we going to have a chance to talk?"

Sterling paused, his hand on the open door. "We'll have plenty of time for that tomorrow. After the race." He waved before he closed the door.

Debra stared at the door for several seconds, already missing his presence. She turned to her mother. "How am I going to live without him?"

"Do you have to?" She grabbed Debra's hand and guided her to the couch Sterling had vacated. "Sit here. Your father wants to talk to you."

Debra lowered herself into the deep cushions and watched as her father shifted nervously on the other end of the long sofa. "Sterling and I talked a lot this week," *Papá* began. "I think maybe you do all this racing for me."

Her breath caught. She clenched her fists at her side. Sterling had gone too far.

"I race because I'm good. I want to win."

He shifted on the couch, moving closer to her. "You don't need to prove that to me. I know you're good."

"But I'm not good in school."

He reached for her fingers and gripped them in his work-roughened hands. "That is my fault."

Debra stilled. She stared at the broken look on his face. A niggle of dread curled down her spine. "How can it be your fault?"

He paused, furrowing his brow and squeezing her fingers tightly. Too tightly. Debra waited, holding her breath.

"When your *mamá* was *embarazada*—pregnant with you— we were in a terrible accident."

Debra's breath caught in her throat. Her stomach tightened. She pulled her hands loose and clenched her fists in her lap, dreading his next words.

"I drank a lot in those days. Your *mamá,* she tell me not to drive the car, but I got mad and made her get in." He dragged his fingers down his craggy face. "We hit a curve too fast, and the car rolled off the road."

His look of agony tore at her heart. Debra grasped his hands, hands that had always seemed so strong.

"You almost died, *mija.* I promised if your life was spared, I would never drink again."

Debra could never remember her father ever taking so much as a sip of alcohol. "You haven't."

"But you still suffer the consequences. Because of the accident, learning is hard for you. It's my fault."

Debra jumped up and began to pace. Suddenly the room didn't seem large. The walls closed in. Tears streaked down her mother's face.

She ran back and planted her feet squarely in front of her father. "Why didn't you tell me this before? I've tried so hard to please you. I was just too stupid to—"

"No, don't say it. You're not stupid." He stood and placed cold, damp fingers on her cheeks. "It is I who am the stupid one. I was so afraid that you wouldn't make it. I couldn't bear the guilt. That's why I pushed you to do well in school."

"Nothing has changed."

"Sterling helped me to understand."

Debra stepped back. "You told him all of this?"

"*Sí, mija.* But you must live for yourself—and for him." He grasped her fingers again and squeezed them. "Not for an old man—*un viejo.*"

Debra held on to her father. Her thoughts spun in a kaleidoscope of emotion. He cared. That was all that mattered. "I love you, *Papá*."

"I love you too, *mi corazón*. I always have." He opened his arms.

Debra stepped into his embrace.

Chapter Seventeen

The hot water soothed her aching muscles, and the almond scent from the bath oil her mother had brought soothed away the throbbing pain in her head. There were so many things to consider—her relationship with Sterling, the enlightenment from her father, the last race. She wanted to close her mind to all of it.

What did it all mean? That Sterling had been right? Her father did indeed love her. Sterling had appeared in her life—a real knight in shining armor. In spite of her accident and maybe even because of it, she was winning in the race of her dreams.

Debra swirled the washcloth in the hot water and covered her chest with the soft material. Warmth crept into her skin as understanding crept into her heart.

A sense of peace washed over her as tears streamed from her eyes. Could it be true? Could *Papá* really care about her? How could she not have known all these years?

Her shoulders shook as the tears flowed. Debra sank down to her chin in the water until she was all cried out. Slowly she stilled, feeling a rebirth as love filled her heart. Could she honor that love? She had to try.

In the morning, all sense of harmony disappeared as she readied for the race. After making hectic arrangements to meet Ralph and Cindy at the staging grounds, she and Sterling left the hotel early. Since her parents were still sleeping, she left a message telling them that she would see them after the race.

During the drive, Sterling discussed strategy, and Debra tried to focus on the event instead of the turmoil of emotions simmering beneath the surface. She wanted to tell Sterling about her new discovery. She wanted to forget the race. She looked at the excitement in his eyes and heard the encouragement in his voice. She couldn't let him down. Or Ralph and Cindy and the team.

She fingered the red, white, and green ribbon her father had given her from his journal. He had told her he was already proud of her. She had to win. To honor that pride. She clenched the ribbon and forced her mind to focus on the day's events.

Because the criterium was staged in the state's capital, there were more spectators than usual. When they arrived, people crowded around the capitol building and lined the streets of the marked-out course. Television news crews struggled to maneuver amid the crowd. Sterling took hold of Debra's arm and pushed his way through the congestion. They found Ralph and Cindy setting up the equipment.

Determined to stay focused, Debra fastened her helmet and balanced her bicycle while Sterling checked the gears and cables. Reminding her of their days together at her parents' home, the steady cadence of his instructions soothed her taut nerves.

He stood and placed his hands on top of hers. "Looks great," he assured her.

She stared into his silver-gray eyes. "I'm going to win."

He leaned over and smiled. "I do believe you are." He winked and adjusted her handlebars.

Debra studied his head bent over her bike and resisted the urge to tangle her fingers in his blond hair. She wanted to beg him to forget the race and take them both away. She longed to tell him she loved him. But her father's ribbon, which she had tied to her handlebars, fluttered in the breeze, and she clenched her fists in readiness.

Cindy stuck Debra's bottles into the cages on her bike. Marilyn went over a few points of strategy. Ralph paced like an expectant father, waiting for the moment the starting gun would get the show on the road.

Debra's nerves hummed like electrical wires. "Shouldn't we head for the starting area?"

Ralph checked his watch, stopping midstride. "Right. Time to head out."

Relief as well as heightened apprehension flooded through Debra. The last event. Soon it would be over, and she could tell Sterling about her love for him. Gripping her handlebars, she glanced up at her beloved. "I'm ready."

Sterling leaned close and whispered, "Remember everything I've taught you."

Debra smiled. "I will." She brushed his cheek with a gloved hand and pedaled to the starting line, where she joined the other cyclists.

Sterling watched with mixed emotions. Debra looked confident and prepped, her kelly green jersey flashing in the sun. He was proud of her courage and stamina, yet he fought an urge to ride with her and protect her against the dangers and pitfalls ahead.

Cindy walked up beside him. "She's going to do it. I can feel it."

"She has what it takes," Sterling agreed, terrified she would win. He wanted her to follow her dream, but after this month away from her, he knew he would pay a huge emotional price if she toured with the Orange-Lites.

"Do you know what this means?" Cindy pointed to the news cameras that followed Debra. "They have her pegged for special attention. Who knows? If she wins, with her looks and charm she could bring women's cycling to the attention of American sports fans."

"Maybe she'll go on to the Olympic trials and sell the public on cycling the way Mary Lou Retton did gymnastics," Ralph commented, hugging Cindy close.

Sterling nodded. "You've got a point." He knew Debra's passion for racing. Sterling needed a goal to pursue also. He couldn't go on the way he had this season, with no fervor for the sport. At least, he hadn't had any enthusiasm until he'd run into Debra.

There had to be a way for them to pursue their dreams together. He'd succeeded with his dream to build a pro team. He'd succeeded in business with his father. He could succeed again with a new goal, a new purpose.

Cindy's voice cut into his thoughts. "She'll make a super role model, won't she?"

"Let's get through this race before we think too far ahead," Ralph advised as he guided them to their seats. "Debra needs to finish without any accidents. Remember *La Vuelta de Bisbee?*"

The reminder of Debra's recent spill sobered all of them. A chill of anxiety coursed down Sterling's neck. Racing always held risks. A cyclist couldn't afford to concentrate on that, however. Victory had to be the focus. He looked at the finish line and pictured Debra crossing it.

Debra rounded a corner and came close to Mary-Reva's rear wheel. She backed off, the pain in her shoulder reminding her of the hazard of getting *too* close. Yet she knew that if she let doubts creep in, she'd lose her edge to win.

At the next straightaway, Debra pulled beside Mary-Reva and tapped her on the knee. Mary-Reva shook her head and held up two fingers, indicating she wanted to wait two more laps before going for a lead-out. Debra nodded.

Hammering around the course, she inwardly chanted, *I can do it. I can do it.*

Finally Mary-Reva signaled Debra. They were in a good position to lead out and break away from the group. If they were lucky, Julie wouldn't notice until it was too late to do anything about it.

When they made their move, their teammates and the crowd lining the street shouted and cheered. Spectators thrived on this type of action. So did Debra. She pedaled with strength she didn't think she had left, pushing herself to the limit.

After the next corner, Debra glanced at Mary-Reva. The breakaway separated them from the pack, but Julie was still with them, holding fast to Mary-Reva's wheel. They'd have to work together to get an advantage over the European star.

"Ready?" Mary-Reva yelled above the noise of the crowd.

Debra nodded. At the next straightaway, she sprinted ahead. Mary-Reva followed on her wheel, ready for a lead-out. Before Julie could react, the two had dusted her. Debra heard a shout of dismay as she hammered to the curve.

This was it. Only the final lap loomed between her and her Orange-Lite nemesis. Mary-Reva had the lead. Debra took advantage of Mary-Reva's draft to catch her breath.

All three women rounded the corner. Time to sprint. Mary-Reva's rear wheel loomed ahead. She had to make a dash now or lose to Mary-Reva. Vivid memories of the crash in Bisbee seized her. Panic set in.

Pain. Weeks of recovery. She couldn't face that again. Perspiration streaked down her face. Or was it tears? Debra gritted her teeth against the pain in her muscles. Her shoulder hurt, but not as badly as her legs. Her lungs burned. A movement caught her eye. Red, white, and green. Her father's ribbon.

Sterling's face came to mind. He had been there with her in spirit through it all. He was here now. "Sterling!" she shouted, even knowing he couldn't hear.

Hammering hard and fast, she pulled out from behind Mary-Reva's wheel. Vaguely she heard the shouts of the crowd as she and Mary-Reva neared the finish line.

Wind whistled through her helmet. Peace washed through her. With jubilation and the last ounce of energy left in her, Debra sprinted across the finish line.

She glanced at Mary-Reva, beside her, neck and neck.

Reaching her fists to the sky, Debra coasted past the capitol building. It didn't matter who had won. She and Mary-Reva had done it. They'd finished the toughest competition in the cycling world for women.

Thanksgiving filled her heart. Winning this race still held tremendous meaning, but she realized it did not compare to love—Sterling's or *Papá*'s.

Gasping for breath, Debra guided her bicycle toward the sidelines. Sterling stood waiting there. When he saw her, he rushed forward, arms in the air.

"You did it! You won!"

Sterling wanted desperately to pull Debra into his arms and run off with her, to shield her from what he knew was coming next. There were no guarantees. She must make her own decisions about her future. But he wasn't so sure that he could watch her walk away from him.

He stood back while Cindy helped Debra off her cycle. Then Ralph grabbed her arm and helped her walk, to keep her muscles from cramping.

In a frenzy of shouts, the crowds and media pressed in. Amid the excitement of the final victory, Debra was carried toward the platform where the officials would announce her win. Sterling felt the cords that had bound them unraveling with each step she took away from him.

She stood on the platform looking more beautiful than he could remember. Wet hair plastered to her head, muscles trembling from strain, and Lycra stained from the road could not detract from the glow in her eyes. An unexpected light of peace in them quickened his heart.

Her voice carried across the crowd, tired but confident. "I want to thank my family for their support and for Ralph and Cindy Robbins of Desert Cyclery for sponsoring me." She searched the crowds until she found him. "I want to thank Sterling Wade, my knight in shining armor, for the training."

The crowd roared and clapped. Laden with flowers, she stepped down from the platform. Sterling fought his way toward her, ready to swing her into his embrace.

Hugh Ashford cut him off and intercepted her. "Congratulations! That was some fine riding today—and these past two weeks, for that matter." He held out his arms for a hug.

She stepped away. "Thank you," she said, peering past Ashford's shoulder to give Sterling a smile.

Sterling tried to step around the team manager but halted when he heard the man's next words.

"The doctors sent us a report this morning about Nancy," Ashford said, referring to the Orange-Lite team member who had crashed during stage two. "She won't be able to ride anymore this season."

"I'm sorry to hear that." Genuine remorse sounded in Debra's voice.

Sterling knew what was coming next but stood powerless to stop it.

"That leaves a vacancy on the team. How would you like to fill it?" Ashford rolled onto the balls of his feet, confident and sure of himself. "You've more than proven your capability and stamina."

The crowd emitted a cacophony of voices and exclamations, but Sterling heard only the silence between Ashford and Debra.

"I'm honored." Debra hesitated, her smile disappearing and her knuckles whitening as she gripped her flowers. "But . . ."

"Think it over. I'd like to make the announcement at the awards ceremony tonight." Ashford pulled a card from his wallet and with a pen from his pocket and began writing. "Here's my cell number. Give me a call before five."

Sterling pictured himself sitting in the Shakespeare Festival Theatre when the final awards were presented, watching his dreams dissolve as Debra's unfolded.

Unable to bear hearing Debra accept the offer, he turned and melded into the crowd.

Debra sidestepped the Orange-Lite manager, ready to fling herself into Sterling's embrace. "Take me out of here, Prince Charming. I'm all done in . . ."

Her words vanished into the wind. Debra spun around. "Sterling?" She stood on tiptoe, looking over the crowd, then she maneuvered her way to Ralph and Cindy. "Where did Sterling disappear to?"

Cindy reached around the flowers and hugged Debra. "Said something about going back to the hotel."

Debra frowned. Why hadn't he waited for her?

Her parents forced their way through the crowd, out of breath and eyes bright with excitement. *Papá* kept his arm around *Mamá*, and with his free hand, he cupped Debra's chin. "*Mija*, you did it."

Joy curled through Debra at the respect and pride in her father's eyes. She'd pleased him, but that knowledge wasn't bringing her the sense of peace she'd thought it would. Sterling had been right.

Peering around her family and friends, she saw the news media approaching, cameras and microphones in hand. But Sterling wasn't anywhere in sight. Fighting disappointment, she braced herself for a barrage of questions and interviews.

Exhausted and yearning to get back to the hotel to find Sterling, Debra pulled Cindy aside. "You heard Ashford's offer?" She rested her head on Cindy's shoulder. "I don't want to leave you and Ralph."

Cindy gave her a squeeze. "We knew all along that this was your goal."

Debra sighed, knowing her friends would not dream of holding her back. She glanced at Ralph as he made his way through the crowd. She owed the two of them so much.

Another hour passed before Debra and her parents stepped

into the hotel elevator. Three o'clock. She didn't have much time before she had to call Ashford.

Her emotions were on a roller-coaster ride. Up and down. Excited and depressed. Confident and undecided. *Sterling.* She needed to talk to him.

Her father opened the door of their room, and Debra stepped inside. "Sterling, we're home." She liked the sound of that. She could picture saying those words every day.

Except she would be on the road with the Orange-Lites. Miles away. Months, weeks, and days away.

Mamá scooted by Debra and started putting the flowers into vases the hotel had provided. Sterling must have notified the staff. Debra smiled at his thoughtfulness.

Her father plopped down onto the sofa, the activity of the day taking its toll. "What is this?" He held a paper he'd picked up off the coffee table. "It's a note from Sterling."

Frowning, Debra grabbed the note and read the familiar handwriting.

My darling Debra,

You have accomplished your dream of touring with the Orange-Lites. I'll miss you, but it's best if I stay away. I don't want to interfere with your goals or jeopardize your position with the team. I'll keep you in my heart, and I'll be waiting . . . always.

Love, Sterling

For long seconds, Debra stared at the handwriting until it blurred through her tears. She gripped the paper so tightly, her fingers turned white. When the reality of his words hit her, she wadded the hotel stationery into a ball and threw it across the room.

"What is it?" *Mamá* hurried to her side.

A sob choked her. "I can't talk now." She ran into her room, slammed the door, and threw herself across the bed. *Why?* Why had he left? Didn't he know she needed him?

Debra reached into her pocket for a Kleenex and pulled out the red, green, and white ribbon. The race and her win flashed through her mind.

She sat upright. She needed Sterling. Needed him. So she would talk to him tonight after the ceremony. Tears streamed down her cheeks. Tears of relief at what she knew, finally, with all her heart. She flopped back onto the bed and let peace wash over her.

Sterling impatiently tapped on the steering wheel of his van as he waited for the light to turn green. A restlessness assailed him. The farther he traveled from the hotel, the more agitated he became. Sweat poured off his brow in spite of the fifty-degree weather. He shifted gears and charged through the intersection. He hadn't felt this edgy since before he'd met Debra.

He'd made the big sacrifice. He should feel at peace. He should feel that he'd made the right decision, but he didn't. Sterling swerved into the parking lot of a corner strip mall and dug in his duffel bag for his cell phone.

After several rings, his father's voice came on the line.

"You have a minute, Dad?" Sterling gripped the cell phone tightly, his fingers aching with the pressure.

"Has Debra been offered a position on a major team?"

His father would have seen the news. Sterling closed his eyes. "Hugh Ashford invited her to join the Orange-Lites. Starting today."

"That was fast. How are you handling it?"

"Not any better than I managed last month." His father had helped him through that miserable time. "I don't know how I'm going to stand being away from her."

"Has it occurred to you that she might feel the same way?" Michael's voice soothed some of the rough edges of Sterling's anguish.

He groaned. "She did miss me, Dad."

"Sounds like you need to come up with a plan."

Sterling squeezed the phone with one hand, rubbing at his

temple with the other. *A plan.* That's what he'd needed all along. Something to get him excited again. Something to stir up his emotions. Something to keep Debra at his side.

He jerked upright out of his slump as an idea began to form. "Dad, I'm quitting the Silverwings for good."

"That team has been your life, son." Surprise sounded in his father's voice.

Sterling shifted the phone to his other ear. "The Silverwings are already established. Joe can manage them without me."

"True." Michael paused, and Sterling could hear papers rustling in the background. "You've been talking about wanting a new goal, a new challenge. Have you something in mind?"

Adrenaline pumped into Sterling's blood as he hashed over ideas with his father.

Michael listened until Sterling had finished brainstorming. "Sounds feasible. Come on home, and we'll iron out the details."

"I have some business to take care of first." Sterling reached for the ignition, eager to get back to the hotel.

"Tell Debra hi from your mother and me." Michael's laughter carried through the phone until Sterling ended the call and slammed the van into gear.

He glanced at the clock on the dash. Four o'clock. If the traffic lights cooperated, he could get to Debra before she called Ashford.

Excitement coursed through him. At the next intersection the light turned red. He shifted restlessly as he waited. He reached for his phone and grabbed his hotel bill to get the number.

"Room nine-forty," he requested.

The traffic light turned green, and he spoke into his hands-free earpiece and shifted gears.

"The line is busy."

Fear trickled down his spine. Four-fifteen. She couldn't be calling Ashford already. Could she?

Every stoplight turned red. Traffic jammed the streets. Sterling gritted his teeth, wishing he could plow through the mess.

At every red light he called the hotel. *Busy. Busy. Busy.*

The clock ticked unmercifully. With each click of the second hand, Sterling could see his dream disappearing from sight.

Five o'clock. Only two blocks. He caught a glimpse of the hotel marquee ahead.

Slamming on the brakes, he jerked the stick shift into park and almost tore the door off in his haste to jump out. He dashed into the lobby.

He held his breath until the elevator doors finally opened on her floor.

"Debra!" He pounded on the solid wood door of the suite.

Her father opened it. Sterling brushed past him. Debra stood near the window, the phone pressed to her ear.

"Debra, don't—"

Her face brightened when she saw him. The phone dropped from her hand. "Sterling, I . . ."

Mamá hurried to pick up the phone and handed it to Debra, who turned her back to Sterling. "Sorry, Hugh. I dropped the phone."

Sterling froze. His heart pounded. Blood flowed against his eardrums with a deafening roar. He wanted to scream, *"No!"*

"As I was saying"—Debra spoke softly but surely—"I can't accept your offer."

Sterling let his breath out in a *whoosh.*

"Why?" She turned and smiled at Sterling. "The reason just walked in the door, so I have to go now. Thanks again for the offer." Debra replaced the receiver and straightened her shoulders.

Relief flooded Sterling. Heart pounding, he lifted her into his arms, spinning her around. "Are you spaced out or what? You just turned down the offer you've been dreaming of."

A gleam of mischief sparkled in her eyes. "Are you disappointed?"

Unable to speak past the lump in his throat, he shook his head. He stopped spinning and set Debra down, but held her close.

Mamá and *Papá* waved to him. "We're going into the other room to get ready."

Sterling and Debra smiled as her parents slipped out the door.

Debra leaned away from him, her smile fading. "I was scared stiff out there today, but I realized something. It was something you taught me."

Sterling fought down a surge of emotion as he gazed into her serious eyes and tried to focus on her words. "What was that?"

Her body quivered as she took a deep breath. "I came to understand that there might be great satisfaction in winning, but peace only comes from knowing you are doing the best you can in whatever circumstances you're in."

Her skin had flushed, darkening its olive tone. Tears glittered in her eyes. Sterling grasped her shoulders, resisting the urge to pull her against his chest. "You can still choose the circumstances," he pointed out. "You love to race."

"But I love you too. You know how Ashford operates. I don't want us to be apart." She placed a hand on his cheek, her fingers warm and steady. Her laugh came from deep in her throat to rustle across his senses.

Sterling's heart pounded as he held his breath. "And you'll have me over a position on a professional team?"

She grinned, light dancing in her dark eyes. "I want you."

Sterling's heart raced with love and anticipation. "What would you say to having both?"

"Both?" Her eyebrows quirked, and she shook back her hair.

He took a deep breath. "As you know, I've been burned out and listless. At least until I met you."

She caressed his cheek. "You need another goal. A new purpose."

"You're right. And you've helped me find it." He pressed a kiss into the palm of her hand. "What about starting our own women's team? You could be our lead cyclist. We know two great coaches, and we already have the beginnings of a team."

Debra straightened, excitement dancing in her eyes. "Ralph and Cindy? Marilyn and the other Desert Roadrunners?"

He nodded.

"That's a fantastic idea. We can call them and start planning now. We can—"

Her excitement delighted him. Pleasure curled down to his toes. "Hold on. We have plenty of time to plan."

His heart pounded. Gently he released her and lifted her chin with one finger. Gazing into her dark eyes, he whispered, "I love you, *querida*. Let's get married and then discuss what we both can have."

"That's one offer I'll accept wholeheartedly," she said as she pulled him to her for a victory kiss.